The Familyman's Christmas Treasury

Todd Wilson

ISBN: 978-1-937639-29-7
Copyright © 2017 Todd Wilson
Illustrations © 2017 Sam Wilson

For more information about Familyman Ministries,
visit familymanweb.com

Printed in the United States of America

Dedicated to

My amazing children, grandchildren, and great grandchildren to come.

May you always know and love the Christ of Christmas.

Love, Dad (& Pops)

TABLE OF CONTENTS

Cootie McKay's Nativity

Book One
of
The Familyman's Christmas Treasury

written and illustrated by
TODD WILSON

1956 was the year of the best Christmas our town ever had. It was also the year we almost didn't have Christmas. But Cootie saved the day. Yes, sir, if it weren't for the talent and vision of Cootie McKay, the folks in our little town would have been mighty disappointed.

You see the problem started a few weeks after the Christmas of '55. We were having lunch one Saturday when my dad got a call from Chet Davis, the town sheriff. My dad wasn't the mayor or anything, he had just lived in the town for so long that people always called him when something big happened. And this was real big.

"Come on, son," my dad said to me, "we got a problem down at the town hall." I wasn't about to miss this one. It could be anything...a boiler explosion, a hostage situation, or a cattle stampede. We only lived about three blocks from the town hall, but we drove our car anyway.

In fact, we were hardly out of the driveway when I noticed the flashing red lights and the crowd that had gathered to see the catastrophe. The crowd parted for my dad's car, and we were shocked by what we saw.

"Shew," was all my dad could say.

I couldn't believe my eyes. Right on the town hall lawn was Mrs. Nichol's '41 Buick. She had smacked into the town nativity just like a bowling ball into the ten pin. Scattered across the lawn and wedged under her car were bits and pieces of the town's nativity scene. It had been a town heirloom for...forever. Until now.

The town nativity was always set in place the weekend after Thanksgiving and wasn't taken down until after the New Year (and sometimes even later if Harley Sheets hadn't cleared out his barn where it was stored).

Mrs. Nichol's was just stepping out of her car when we pulled up. She was as old as dirt itself. Dad told me she was something like 123 when he was a kid. Everyone knew she shouldn't be driving anymore, and if you saw her big blue Buick coming down the road, you got behind the nearest tree if you had any sense at all.

"Oh, this is bad," Sheriff Davis said as he walked up to my dad, "real bad."

"Now, calm down Chet. Is Mrs. Nichol's all right?"

"All right? She doesn't even know that she's ruined Christmas for the whole town." The sheriff slapped himself in the forehead.

We walked over to Mrs. Nichols.

"What seems to be the problem, Officer?" she asked, bothered by the commotion. I hadn't been that close to Mrs. Nichols before, and I was shocked by how many wrinkles she had. She really was older than dirt.

"Mrs. Nichols, are you OK?" my dad asked.

"Why, I'm fine. I was just on the way to the post office to mail this Christmas package to my son out in Arizona..."

"Yes, Mam, but were you hurt in the accident?"

"Accident?" she asked in a panic. "Was there an accident?"

Chet interrupted, overcome by emotion, "You ran over the nativity, Mam! Look, a camel is wedged under your car."

"Well, why did they set it up in the parking lot this year?" she asked, irritated by his accusation. "It seems like you're just asking for trouble if you set it up in a parking lot..."

"This is not a parking lot, Mam." Chet fired back.

"Well, then why are all these cars parked here?"

Dad interrupted before Mrs. Nichols and Sheriff Davis could get in a fistfight. Dad was afraid Sheriff Davis would lose.

"Why don't we have someone drive Mrs. Nichols home and then...?"

"But I have to mail this package to my son in Arizona. If I don't, it won't be there in time for Christmas."

Dad didn't have the heart to tell her that she had already missed Christmas by three weeks. Instead, they took her to the post office to mail her package and then to her home, while they untangled the three wise men from her bumper.

Later that night, an impromptu town meeting was held at our house. I was supposed to be in bed, but I could hear real well through the heating vent in my room.

"So, what's the damage, Ed?" my dad asked Ed Jacobson, the town maintenance guy.

"Well, about the only pieces that aren't broken are two sheep and a cow.

The three wise men are now the twenty-six-pieces-of wisemen, and Mary, Joseph, and Jesus were pounded flatter than a pancake. We might fix the angel of the Lord, but it won't be easy. As far as the shepherds, camels, and the other animals go, we had to sweep them up with a dustpan."

Chet Davis moaned in agony.

"Well, what are we going to do?" Dean Baker asked. He was the town treasurer. "We don't have any money in the budget to spend on a new nativity. I heard Millersburg bought a new set two years ago, and it cost over a thousand dollars."

"Well, we've got to do something," Betty Acton added. "All the other towns have a nativity scene, and we're not going to be the only town in Indiana not to have a nativity."

The others agreed but were at a loss as to what to do. They talked well over an hour without any solution. In frustration, Chet Davis said, "There's no way. It can't be done."

"How about Cootie McKay?" my dad mentioned out of the blue.

Ten seconds of nerve jiggling silence passed. I even thought I heard Dean Baker's false teeth slide out of his mouth and onto the table.

"Cootie?!" Chet gasped. "Why would we ask Cootie?"

Cootie McKay was just about the oddest person you'd ever meet. He rode an orange bicycle with a purple basket mounted up front. He rode down Main

Street at least twenty-five times a day, with his shirt buttoned up to the top button, a heavy wool jacket on (even in the middle of the summer), wearing two mismatched shoes.

He hardly ever talked to anyone, but I always wondered if that was because no one ever talked to him. Sometimes at night he'd sit in a tree in his yard, hooting like an owl. I knew that, because his house was across the alley, right behind ours.

He lived alone ever since his mother died. The yard was filled with trash and had been the reason for several town meetings. His real name was Thomas McKay, but everyone called him Cootie.

Cootie had a talent for converting old car parts, sinks, and scrap wood into art. That's why my dad thought of him.

"You know, he really has made some pretty neat things out in his yard," my dad offered.

Mrs. Acton rolled her eyes at the thought of Cootie making their nativity.

"Yeah, maybe he could make the manger out of a toilet," Chet hooted. "I can't believe you would even think about asking Cootie."

The others agreed.

"I bet he's never even read about the birth of Jesus," someone said.

"He sure doesn't go to church, and he probably has never opened a Bible," Mrs. Acton added.

"Well, do you have a better idea?" Dad asked.

They tried real hard to come up with a better idea but couldn't.

"OK," my dad said, "I'll talk to Cootie then. Besides, if it's terrible, we don't have to put it out."

The meeting was over, and they all went home with the thought that Christmas, as our town knew it, was over.

Three days later, right after dinner, Dad announced that he was going over to Cootie's house.

"Can I go with you?" I asked.

My mom shot Dad a glance to let him know she wasn't really excited about the idea.

"Why…uh…sure you can go," he said.

Mom smiled reluctantly. "Go on," she said.

A few minutes later we were at Cootie's, waiting for him to answer the door. The front porch was covered with junk. A huge grizzly bear made completely out of smashed pop cans guarded the door, while a turtle created from a hubcap sat next to the milk box.

"I guess he's not home," Dad said after several attempts. "I could have sworn I saw him working out front before dinner."

We turned to leave, when a voice spoke out of nowhere, "Can I hep you?"

We looked around, but there was no Cootie.

"Hello, Cootie?" Dad called, "Where are you?"

"I'm right here," he said from a tall tree that over-shadowed the porch.

We stepped out into the middle of the yard and saw Cootie, perched up in the tree like a squirrel. He had a plate of spaghetti on his lap and was sucking a long noodle from his fork with a slurp.

"Yeah, Cootie," Dad started nervously, "we were wondering if you could help us out?"

"I will ifin I can," he answered softly, never stirring from his perch.

"I don't know if you heard about the town nativity set..."

Cootie was silent.

"Probably doesn't know what a nativity is," I thought.

"We've got a problem. We were wondering...uh, if you could build us a new nativity?"

Cootie didn't move so much as a muscle. He didn't even look at my dad. He was stone still. Dad was about to repeat the whole thing when a big, gray squirrel jumped from a branch and scrambled up Cootie's arm, grabbing a crust of bread from his hand.

"So, do you think you could do it?" my dad continued.

Cootie stroked the underside of the squirrel's chin. "I can try, "he said, "but I don't know nuttin' about a nativ...ity."

"Ha! I was right," I thought.

"You saw the one on the town hall lawn, didn't you?"

"Yep, but I aint never did understood it."

"Maybe when you're not so busy," Dad said, "you could stop over at our house, and I can tell you what we were thinking."

"Sure," was all he said. Just then two more squirrels raced up the trunk and onto his lap.

"Well, we'll see you...uh...sometime."

Dad shrugged his shoulders, and we walked away silently.

My dad nodded his head in disbelief. "Oh, man," he whispered.

"So, when do you think he'll come over?" I asked on our way home.

"Who knows? I heard he sometimes sleeps in that tree for days."

Dad laughed and threw his hand on my shoulder. "Well, let's see if your mother has any dessert on the table."

We'd been in the house for less than two minutes when a knock came at the door.

Looking up from the pie, mom said, "I wonder who that is?"

I ran to the door, never expecting it to be Cootie McKay, but there he was standing outside with spaghetti sauce dabbled around the edges of his mouth, a tennis shoe on his left foot, and an army boot on the other.

"I'm here," he said.

He certainly was.

Over a piece of cherry pie, Dad tried to explain the idea of a nativity to Cootie. He brought out his Bible and read about the birth of Jesus, the shepherds in the field, and the wisemen and their gifts.

Cootie rubbed his hand over his grizzled chin and scrunched his eyebrows together deep in thought. He soaked up every word and nodded thoughtfully. It took two hours to explain the story, the project, and what they wanted from him. At the end my dad asked, "Do you have any questions, Cootie?"

Cootie pondered the question for several seconds. "Can I have yur book?" he said, pointing to the Bible in my father's lap.

"Sure. You can take this home with you." He handed the Bible to Cootie, and Cootie stood to leave.

"When do ya need that 'thing'?" he asked, studying the cover of the Bible.

"It needs to be set up the day after Thanksgiving."

Cootie gave his head a nod and left with the Bible under his arm and cherry pie AND spaghetti sauce dabbled around the edges of his mouth.

For the next three weeks things were quiet. We didn't see much of Cootie. Then one night, a knock came at the door, and it was him.

Dad answered, and before he could say, "Hi, Cootie," Cootie was sitting at our table with his Bible opened.

"So, this Mary and Joseph couldn't find no place for their baby to be borned and had to stay in a barn?"

It took Dad a second to get his bearings but when he did, he answered, "Yeah. There was a census taken and uh...all the uh...hotels were full."

"But it sez he'z God's Son. Why would they make him be borned in a barn?" Cootie looked troubled.

"I don't know, but that's the way it was."

Cootie held up the Bible and asked, "And then that Herod guy wanted to kill him. Why'd he wanna do that?"

"Because he didn't want any other King taking his place," my dad explained.

Cootie thought for a while, nodded his head, and said, "Oh." Then he left.

Night after night, Cootie came to our house. He'd ask questions about the Bible, look perplexed, and then leave.

When he talked about the angel and the shepherds, he laughed the loudest, funniest laugh I had ever heard. It sounded like a bird was caught in his throat.

"I betcha those shepherd guys wuz scared to deaf when them angels came. I aint never did see an angel. But I'd be scared ifin I did."

It got to the point where we looked forward to the time after dinner when Cootie would come walking in our door. He quit knocking after two weeks. He just walked right in, sat down at the table, and asked his questions.

When he wasn't asking questions, he was banging in his house or rummaging through his junk piles, like a hound dog looking for a rabbit. Many times I'd see him riding his bike, pulling a cart full of new junk home.

By spring, he finished reading about the birth of Jesus and went on to all His miracles and His run-ins with the Pharisees.

"Boy, them Pharisee guys iz nasty critters. They got their nosez all bent 'cuz Jesus sez He's God." Cootie got red in the face. "I'd like to hav taken a stick to 'em."

"And how cum that John feller called Jesus the Lamb of God?" Cootie asked.

Dad explained how back then a lamb was killed as a sacrifice for sin.

"That's the dumbest thing I've ever heard," Cootie said, shaking his head at the mere thought of Jesus looking like a sheep.

One hot June night, Dean Baker stopped by on his way to the Dairy Bar for an ice cream cone.

"Have you seen any of the nativity pieces yet?" he asked my dad.

"No, but Cootie comes over every night to talk about it. I tell you what, he knows the story better than I do."

"That's all good and fine, but what's it going to look like?"

"I don't know, Dean. He doesn't want to show it to anyone until it's finished."

"Well, make him. Tell him we won't pay him until he does."

"He doesn't even know we are going to pay him. He's never asked."

Truth was no one knew how Cootie lived. He didn't have a job. Apparently, his mother left him money, and he didn't need to work.

Dean Baker left in a huff, muttering something about 'Cootie ruining Christmas.'

The summer passed, while the piles of junk outside Cootie's house shrunk and the endless banging lessened. Everyone on the town board was getting nervous, afraid that their nativity scene was going to be the laughing stock of the state – maybe even the country.

"We'll probably be on the national news," Sheriff Davis said. "I can see the headlines now: See the toaster in the manger."

Dad tried to reassure them, but he wasn't so sure himself. They were, after all, putting the fate of the town's Christmas in the hands of the man who just last week was seen pulling a pink bathtub down the center of Main Street.

Then something odd happened. The table had been cleared, and Mom had set out dessert, including a piece for Cootie, when a knock came at the door.

That was surprising, because Cootie hadn't knocked at the door for six months. I opened the door and found Cootie in tears. His eyes were red and puffy, and his hair was a mess—even for him. I knew something was bad wrong when I saw that his shoes matched, because I'd never seen Cootie wear matching shoes.

He didn't say a word; just walked in, put his Bible on the table and said, "They killed him."

"Killed who, Cootie?" Dad asked.

"They killed Jesus." Cootie brought his hands to his face and burst into

tears. "I can't believe they killed Him," he repeated. "He'd never dun nuttin' wrong."

Dad tried to comfort him, but nothing he said helped.

"Just keep reading," Dad said.

Instantly, Cootie stopped, and then like always, got up and left.

Bright and early the next morning, Cootie stood on our porch, pounding on the front door with all his might. "He didn't stay dead!" he shouted through the closed door. "Jesus is alive!!"

By the time Dad stumbled to the door, Cootie had gone back home, only to return an hour later to tell us again that Jesus was alive.

Of course, we already knew it, but it was all a surprise to Cootie, and he looked like he had been given the world. Over and over he kept repeating, "Can you believe dat? Jesus didn't stay dead. Of course, He didn't," he'd answer himself, "He'z God."

After that day, Cootie disappeared—not all together, mind you. He just didn't come to our house anymore. The banging and sawing in his house turned up to full speed. Day and night he worked, stopping only long enough to feed his squirrels or get some more junk for his project.

Dad and I went over one Saturday afternoon about the middle of November and knocked on his door. Dad was anxious and wanted to know how Cootie was coming along on the town nativity. When he didn't answer the door, we had to go home to sweat it out.

There were only eleven days left.

Those were long days. Several of the town board members stopped by to see how things were coming. They were all told the same thing, "I don't know." There was no plan B, no turning back now. Christmas was up to Cootie McKay.

Thanksgiving was terrible. Most of the town got indigestion from worrying about the next day. We invited Cootie over for a special meal, but he said he had too much work to do on the nativity.

"We're sunk," Dad whispered to Mom, "and I'm gonna be blamed for this. He probably isn't even close to being finished...and even if he is, it will probably be terrible—yep, I'm sunk."

Mom tried to encourage him, but it didn't work.

That night, no one at our house slept. I propped a pillow by my bedroom window overlooking Cootie's house. It was mostly dark and quiet, with just a few shadows of movement and whispers...

I fell asleep on the cold floor under the window, waking at 6:48 A.M.

"Today's the day," I thought. Dad said we'd go down to see the nativity right after breakfast, but I was barely out of bed before the phone rang.

"No, I haven't seen the nativity yet," my dad said into the phone. "Yes, I'll be right down." He hung up the phone and gave an odd look toward my mother. The phone rang again.

"Yes, mam," he said, "Cootie made it...no, I haven't seen it yet." He hung up. The phone rang again, then again, and again.

Each time a voice on the other end asked if Dad had seen the nativity and if Cootie made it. After that, they just held the phone in silence. "It's probably so horrible that they're speechless," Dad said, as he threw on his coat. "Come on," he said to Mom and me, "let's get this over with."

We decided to walk this time. I think Dad thought it would prolong the inevitable. If it hadn't been the nativity unveiling, it would have been a beautiful morning. The sun was just rising, and the windows sparkled down Main Street.

The entire town was out this morning. They were all headed to the town hall lawn, drawn like moths to a lantern. By the time we got there, it was so packed that we couldn't even see the nativity scene.

It was the strangest sight I ever saw. Cars had been left right in the middle of the street with their doors still wide open, bicycles were dropped on the sidewalk, and even Jack Helfer's tow truck sat in the middle of the intersection, still towing a beat-up wreck.

"Oh boy, it must really be bad," I thought.

We wound our way through the crowd up to the front, and then we saw it: Cootie McKay's nativity.

Sheriff Davis stood next to us with his mouth dropped open. He didn't even see us join him. Seconds later we didn't see him either. All we could see was the miracle before us. That's what those on the town board called the nativity from then on—the miracle.

It was indescribable. Even the words on this page can't begin to describe what I saw that morning.

It was the most beautiful nativity ever made. You could look at it for hours, then turn away for five seconds, turn back, and it was as though you were looking at it for the very first time.

In a way, it seemed to be moving. I don't know how Cootie did it, but the animals seemed to be swaying back and forth, the shepherds looked like they were running, even the robes of the wise men seemed to sway in the wind, but there was no wind.

I said 'seemed,' because on closer examination, it was obvious that none of them could move. They had been made from steel, iron, and wood, and probably weighed more than a ton a piece. They were made from Cootie's junk. Five life-size camels were made from crushed cans, like his grizzly bear. Their eyes were fishing lures, and their ears were leather shoes.

The shepherds were made from bent, welded steel and iron that looked as soft as silk blowing in a summer breeze. It wasn't until the third year that I noticed that their fingers were made from typewriter keys, and their sandals were made from license plates.

Every single piece of the nativity was made from regular, old, broken, discarded junk. Even more amazingly was the way they stood and the look on their faces. It was so different and yet so—right.

Cootie's shepherds looked like they had run all the way to the town hall lawn. The first one to arrive was bent over and out of breath. His sides looked like they were going in and out, which like I said earlier, was impossible—I think. Other shepherds looked like they were laughing, overjoyed with the news of the Savior's birth. Their eyes sparkled with hope and wonder. Somehow they looked overwhelmed to have been picked to receive the angel's message.

Scattered here and there were angels. They weren't your everyday variety of angels with little wings and diapers on. They were soldiers of shining steel, with swords and shields that flashed like mirrors. Their fiery eyes seemed to scan the crowd, protectively guarding the child in the manger. Their stern faces kept the crowd at a safe distance.

In the middle were Joseph and Mary. Joseph stood next to the manger with his arms crossed over his chest. He looked proud and protective, brave yet scared. He was made mostly of wood, which had been carved from a large log. Bark clung to his back and sides like a rough robe.

Mom thought Cootie made him from wood because he had been a carpenter. Interestingly enough, his hands were made from chisels, hammers, and saws.

Mary sat next to him on a rough bench, made from an upside down bathtub. She was smiling, but looked tired and worn out and leaned back heavily on her arms. She was made from rusted sheet metal but looked as young and fragile as a young girl. Her deep brown eyes peered lovingly into the manger.

The most shocking part came from inside the manger. It was...a baby lamb,

like a sheep. No one knew what it was made of. It looked as much like a new-born lamb—as a newborn lamb. Against its snowy white head was a wreath of rusted needle-sharp nails. They bit into its flesh and rust (or blood) trickled down his face.

People smiled and cried as they looked upon the lamb. A few turned and left in silence. The town could have burst into flames, and no one would have noticed.

For several minutes, no one spoke. Then slowly, people started to whisper and point. Then they laughed and shook their heads in amazement. Some went home, only to return an hour later.

Sheriff Davis turned to my dad and started to speak, but he couldn't. There were tears in his eyes, his lip quivered, and his cheeks twitched. He finally just shook his head and walked away. Others looked at my Dad and smiled. Some folks offered thanks and congratulations.

"Oh," Dad said, "I didn't do anything. Cootie did it all."

It was then that we noticed that Cootie wasn't anywhere to be seen. Dad asked a few of the men in the crowd if they had seen him, but no one had seen Cootie all morning.

On our way home, we walked in silence, thinking about what we saw. A car pulled up along side us, and Dean Baker stuck his head out the window.

"I knew Cootie could do it. Didn't I tell you he could do it? I wouldn't be surprised if people from all over the state come to see our nativity."

Dad just nodded and smiled.

Once home, Dad said, "I'm going over to see if Cootie is home."

Mom went inside, and I begged to go with my dad. At the front door we pounded, and like usual, he didn't answer.

"I hope it's OK," a voice said from above us.

I turned to see Cootie up in his tree, with one squirrel on his head and another eating from his hand.

"Cootie," Dad said, "it's perfect." This time my dad's lip quivered, and his eyes filled with tears.

"Good. I'm glad ya like it."

We stood there for a few minutes, and no one spoke. Finally, Dad turned to leave.

"We'll expect you for dessert tonight," he said over his shoulder.

Cootie smiled, and we made our way back home. We had just crossed the alley when Cootie called out to my dad.

"What is it, Cootie?" he asked.

Cootie had jumped out of the tree and all we could see of him were his arms above his head. And then Cootie shouted, "Jesus aint dead no more. He'z alive!"

The End

Book Two
of
The Familyman's Christmas Treasury

written and illustrated by
TODD WILSON

rendering by SAM WILSON, *staging by* BEN, KAT, & IKE WILSON

"The night was calm as the baby lay in the manger. Shepherds bowed before the King. All was silent, when…**BAM**!!! **Out of the darkness, like a blaze of fire, came *Captain Chaos*, defender of the universe, with his trusty manger blaster!"**

"You're kidding, right?" Martha Ann asked. "There's no Captain Chaos in the Bible story."

"Well, there should be," answered Jason. "The story is so boring; it needs something to make it more exciting."

"You can't just go and change the story of Christmas," Martha Ann argued.

"Why not? I think I could tell a better story than the Bible," Jason countered. "Captain Chaos fires his retro rockets and lands in a cloud of dust in front of the manger…" Jason imagined outloud.

"Stop it," Martha Ann hollered. "If you don't stop, I'm going to tell Mom what you're doing."

"Just try it earth girl, and I'll blast you into space dust," Jason said mechanically.

That was it. Martha Ann got up and raced to the kitchen. A minute later she returned, with their mother right behind her.

"What is going on in here, Jason?" Mom asked.

"Nothing," Jason answered, "we were just having fun..."

"He's changing the whole story," Martha interrupted. "Jason said the Bible story isn't exciting enough..."

"It's not. I've heard it a million times, and I just thought I could make it a little better—that's all," Jason answered.

"See, I told you he was trying to ruin it," Martha Ann said proudly.

"Jason," his mother began, "you can't change the Bible story. That's the way it really was."

"But it's boring..." Jason whined.

"I don't want to hear another word, young man. If you can't tell it right, then go to your room and go to bed right now," Jason's mom scolded. Martha Ann squinted her eyes at her brother and smiled.

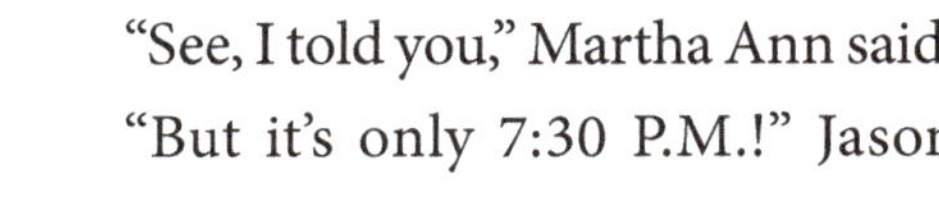

"See, I told you," Martha Ann said.

"But it's only 7:30 P.M.!" Jason pleaded.

"You heard me," his mother warned.

"Fine, then I won't play," Jason said as he got up, grabbed Captain Chaos, went to his room, and shut Martha Ann and the rest of the world out.

"Dumb story," he mumbled under his breath. "I don't care

if I ever hear about the manger again."

Jason put his pajamas on, and he and Captain Chaos jumped into bed with a thump, hoping everyone on the other side of his bedroom door had heard it.

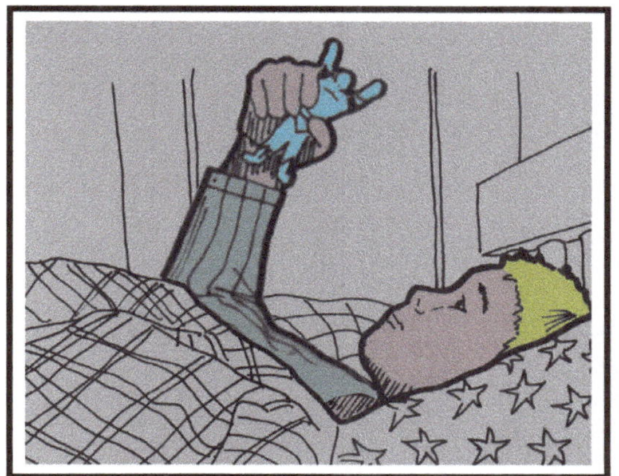

"See if I care about going to bed early," he muttered. "I didn't want to play anymore with the silly old manger anyway." Jason didn't even say his prayers that night. He just stared at the ceiling and flew Captain Chaos over his head, pretending to land him on the craggy surface of his bed.

Just how long he played, he wasn't sure, but as he lay in bed, he noticed that his bedroom window grew

bright. He glanced at the clock.

"It's 11:30 P.M. Why is it so light outside?" he wondered. The light grew brighter, and Jason moved to the foot of his bed to look out.

At first, he thought the bright light was the moon, but then he realized it was too bright for that. And it was getting closer every second.

"What is that?" he thought. "A plane, a shooting star, a meteorite?"

Whatever it was, it was headed straight for his house, roaring like a rocket engine. Jason slammed his hands over his ears and ran to his door. Before he reached it, the light crashed through his bedroom wall with a HUGE EXPLOSION, blasting his bed into a MILLION PIECES!!

Jason threw himself to the floor, expecting the house to collapse any second. When it didn't, he opened his eyes.

A gaping hole blackened his bedroom wall and a tall muscular man in metallic blue armor stood in the middle of his room. A helmet covered his face, but his eyes glowed green through the mask.

Wisps of smoke curled from two rockets strapped to his back, and he scanned the room.

"Are you Jason?" asked the man in a deep, mechanical voice.

Jason was unable to speak and only nodded nervously.

"I've come to help you," he said.

"Who...who are you?" Jason sputtered.

"I...am Captain Chaos."

By this time, Jason had returned to his senses and was surprised that his parents and sister hadn't come running into the room after the house-jarring collision.

"Why are you here?" he asked Captain Chaos.

"I told you, I'm here to help you. Did you not say you wish you could get rid of the manger?"

The words sounded like his. "Yeah…"

"Well, I can do that."

"You're kidding, right?"

"*I never kid*," he said coldly, "*it's against space hero regulations*."

"Wow, I didn't know that."

"Now you do."

Captain Chaos picked up a large chunk of bedroom wall, tossed it aside with ease, and set a large 'rocket looking thing' on the floor.

"What is that?" Jason asked, stepping closer.

"It's a standard issue Universe Altering Blaster." As he spoke, he pressed a glowing red button on the side of it. Instantly, the machine began to hum. Three spider-like legs shot from its side, the top cover opened, and a clear shaft of green glass rose from the opening.

"Jason, I need to ask you to stand back from the eradicator as I set it for detonation." He leaned over a touch pad located on the side of the machine and punched a few keys. "We now have thirty seconds until manger-eradication," he said calmly.

"What do you mean, manger eradication?" Jason asked.

"It is as you wanted. In twenty-two seconds, the manger will be eliminated from the planet."

"I don't want that."

"You did say that, didn't you?"

"Yeah, but I didn't mean..."

"Then I was correct." Captain Chaos looked at the display and stepped back. "Detonation will occur in twelve seconds."

"No," shouted Jason above the whirling hum. At ten seconds, the glass shaft began to pulse with light, and the floor began to quake. "Stop it!"

"I'm afraid it's too late.
You might want to plug your ears for this one…7,6,5,4,3,2,1…"

In the next instant, there was a terrific flash of light, and the air was sucked from the room. Jason felt like he was floating as the blaster sucked in everything around him. A second later, it was over.

Jason found himself lying in bed as he had when the night started. Captain Chaos was gone, the hole in the bedroom wall was gone…everything was just like normal, except that it was morning.

"Whoa, it must have been a dream," Jason said to himself. "That was weird."

Just then his mom called, "Come on, Jason, time for breakfast."

Jason threw his clothes on and ran down to the kitchen table.

"That was quick," she said. "Did you sleep OK?"

"I guess," he answered. She set a bowl of cereal before him, and he bowed his head to pray."

"You asleep?" his mother asked. She walked over and shook his shoulder lovingly.

"I'm praying," he said.

"Praying? Why would you do that?" she looked confused by the explanation.

"We always pray before we eat," Jason said, wondering

if she was joking.

"We do, huh? Well, I don't remember us ever doing that." She raised an eyebrow in his direction, "Who you praying to?"

"Jesus, who else?"

"Jesus? That's a new one on me. Is he another one of your superheroes?" Before he could answer, she walked out of the room. As she did, Martha Ann walked in, wearing pink fuzzy pajamas.

"Why aren't you dressed yet? We're supposed to get our Christmas tree today, remember?"

She looked at him skeptically. "Christmas tree? What's a Christmas tree?"

"What do you mean, 'What's a Christmas tree?' Your brain still asleep?"

"Ha ha, very funny. I'm laughing."

As Jason sat eating his cereal, their mother walked back into the now silent room.

"Mom, I'm worried about Martha Ann. She can't remember what a Christmas tree is."

"She's not the only one," his mother said dryly. "So, what's a Christmas tree?"

"You're kidding, right?" he asked, his mouth full of cereal.

"*I never kid,*" she said, "*it's against mother regulations.*"

"Oh, come on, Mom. Stop it."

"Stop what?"

"So, neither of you know what a Christmas tree is?"

Martha Ann and his mother looked at him blankly.

"You know, Christmasssss?

"No, we don't know Christmasssss," she said. "Remind us."

"You know Santa Claus and presents?"

"Who's Santa Claus?"

"He's the guy who lives at the North Pole, drives a sled with flying reindeer..."

"Oh, boy, I think he's lost it, Mom."

"Martha Ann, don't," scolded her mother. "He's just teasing."

Jason was starting to get frustrated by the conversation.

"I'm not teasing. Come on; stop it. OK, I give up. I'm sorry for last night and the manger thing."

"What manger thing?" Martha Ann asked.

"I'm sorry for making fun of Jesus and the

manger story."

"What do you mean?" she asked. "What manger story, and who is Jesus?"

"Stop it!" he shouted. "You know all about Jesus, the manger, and Christmas."

His mother looked at her

son with concern in her eyes. "Sorry, honey, we don't know what you're talking about. We're trying, but you're going to have to explain it again." Jason could tell this was no joke. They really had no idea what he was talking about.

"Where's Dad? He'll understand."

"He's not here. Mr. Duncan died yesterday, and he went over to see Mrs. Duncan."

Mr. Duncan lived a few houses down and had been sick for a while.

"Was he a Christian?" Jason asked.

"What's a Christian?" Martha Ann said.

"Don't start that. You know what a Christian is."

"I don't either. I've never even heard of a Christian..."

"STOP!!! You've been a Christian since you were six. Remember? I was there when you asked Jesus into your heart."

Both Martha Ann and his mother looked at Jason like worms were crawling out of his nose.

"I've never done that," Martha Ann said, "and I'm not a Christian."

"Then how do you expect to get to heaven?"

Her face grew grim. "I don't," she said softly.

"None of us do, honey," his mother added. "That's just the way it is."

"NO! I don't believe you." Jason got up from the table and ran into the living room. He looked to where the nativity scene sat, and it wasn't there. Then an idea came to him, and he ran down to the basement.

He flipped on the light and pushed aside a sack of clothes.

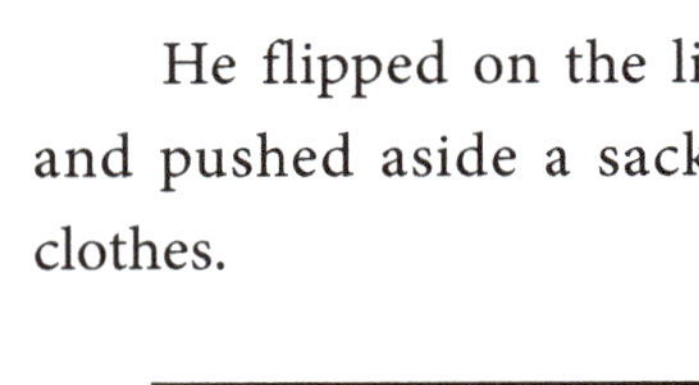

The Christmas decorations weren't there. They should have been there. They were always there. Instead, the spot was filled with paint cans.

"Someone must have moved them," he thought.

Jason ran upstairs and into the kitchen. "You moved them, didn't you?" he accused his sister.

She shrugged her shoulders in ignorance.

"I'm going out," he called on his way out the door.

"Make sure you're back for dinner," his mother called back. She looked at Martha Ann and sighed.

Peddling as fast as he could, Jason rode for town, which was less than a mile away.

"I'll prove it to them," he told himself.

Coming into town was like a bad dream. The holiday greenery that usually hung from the streetlights was missing. There were no lights on the buildings or Christmas decorations in the windows.

Desperate, he walked into Murphy's Department Store.

"It's always decorated for Christmas," he thought.

This time it wasn't.

There wasn't even a single strand of tinsel anywhere in the store.

Thinking it was all some kind of elaborate joke, he went to the cashier and asked, "Yeah, can you tell me where your Christmas decorations are?" Jason tried to look calm as he waited for her answer.

"Just a second," she answered and walked across to another cashier. "Do we have any Christmas decorations?" she asked.

"No," the other woman answered and then added, "What are Christmas decorations?"

"Beats me," she said and turned to ask Jason, but he was already out the door and on his bike.

"This is too weird," he thought.

As he reached the library, he noticed something else was missing—the Presbyterian Church.

There was a brick house in its place.

A dreadful thought came over Jason, and he rode his bike a couple of blocks to where the Baptist Church should have been. It wasn't there either. Minutes later, he discovered that they were all missing…

the Method- ist Church,

the Pentecostal Church,

even the ornate Catholic Church.

They were all gone.

Jason felt panicky, rode back to Murphy's, and walked back up to the same cashier.

"I'm looking for a gift for my mother and was wondering if you have any cross necklaces."

She looked unsure and walked over to the other cashier who was organizing some shelves, whispered, and then returned.

"What kind of cross were you looking for?"

"You know, a Christian cross... the kind Jesus was crucified on?"

"We're not really sure what those are, but we don't have any of them."

"You're kidding," Jason   accused.

"*No sir, I never kid, it's against cashier regulations.*"

Jason walked out of the store and spent the rest of the afternoon riding around in search of Christmas, but it was nowhere to be found. Christmas was gone.

When evening came, he gave up and went home. He was convinced. Captain Chaos had eradicated the manger and obliterated Christmas. Without the manger, there were no decorations, no Santa Claus, and no nativities. And even worse, there were no churches, no cross, no Jesus, and no way to heaven.

Without the manger, there was no hope.

Back at home, Jason collapsed on his bed and stared at the blank ceiling. Then a thought came to him. It was such a simple thought that he almost did nothing about it.

"It won't be there," he told himself.

But something

deep inside him urged him to check anyway. He got out of bed and walked slowly towards his dresser. He was afraid to look and face yet another disappointment, but he had to look just the same.

Slowly, he opened the top drawer and slid his hand under a stack of T-shirts.

He felt a book but was afraid to pull it out.

What if he was wrong? He couldn't put it off any longer. He removed the book from the drawer, and when he did, a wave of relief poured over him.

It was his Bible, the one his mom and dad had given him for his birthday. His name was written on it in small gold letters. Jason took the Bible back to his bed and quickly opened it to Luke 2:6 and read these words:

"While they were

there, the time came for the baby to be born, and she gave birth to her firstborn, a son. She wrapped him in cloths and placed him in a manger, because there was no room for them in the inn.''

The words sounded good to his ears, but before there was time to get too emotional, a terrific flash filled the room. The air rushed all around him toward the center of the room, like water down a drain. It sucked so hard that it peeled the paint from the wall and ripped up the floor boards.

A moment later, the last bit of light vanished into the floor, leaving behind an object whirling on the ground like a coin. Then it came to a stop.

Jason walked toward the object. It was Captain Chaos. He looked at the tiny superhero and then at the clock on his nightstand. It was 7:46 P.M.

He jumped up from the

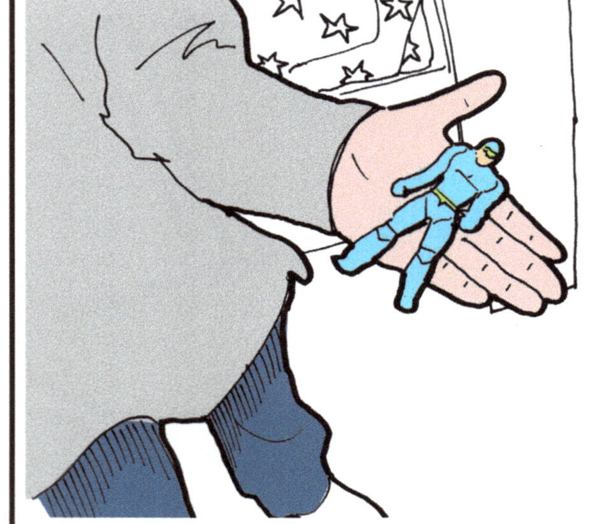

floor and ran downstairs.

"You decide to stay up?" Martha Ann

called to him. She was still playing with the nativity set in the living room. "You want to play, or is this too boring for you?"

"Sure, I'll play. I think it's the greatest story ever."

Martha Ann looked at him and wondered what happened to the kid who had stomped upstairs just a few minutes ago.

"You're kidding, right?" she asked.

Jason smiled knowingly. "*I never kid,*" he said, "*it's against brother regulations.*"

The End

The Stranger

Book Three
of
The Familyman's Christmas Treasury

written and illustrated by
TODD WILSON
(with the help of Sam Wilson)

Every Christmas Eve, people gather in churches, big and small, to celebrate the birth of Christ. Bells are rung, candles are lit, *Silent Night* is sung, and memories are made. For nine-year-old Sam Tucker, it is his favorite night of the year.

But one year, the year of the big snow, people seemed out of sorts because a stranger had come to town.

The Christmas Eve service was about to begin when Mr. Fisher, one of the church deacons, spoke up. "I don't know what we're going to do," he announced abruptly to all the surprised faces. "The stranger came to our door last night.

"You didn't let him in, did you, Norm?" Walt Mitchell interrupted.

"Well, of course I didn't let him in," Mr. Fisher shot back. "Do you think I'm crazy? I hollered through the door and told him to get off our porch," he said in the bravest voice he could muster. People in the small sanctuary gasped, and Mr. Fisher added, "He didn't say a word; just turned and left."

"He showed up at my house three nights ago," Mrs. Johnson said. "I was so scared I locked myself in the bathroom 'til morning. I'm still a nervous wreck."

"He stopped at our house a week ago," a man in the back of the room yelled.

"Mine, too!" a voice piped in.

By this time the lights had been turned up, and it felt more like a basketball game than a Christmas Eve service. All around the room, people told their stories. It seemed that the stranger had appeared at all of their homes.

"Funny thing about it," Mr. Teeple shouted above the roar, "is I've been asking around town, and no one else seems to have seen or heard of him— just the folks in our church."

If people weren't scared up until that moment, they were then. Some talked about getting the sheriff involved, and others said they were leaving town to stay with relatives. Panic was about to erupt when Pastor Martin stood to speak.

"Settle down everyone," he said in a deep voice. "It's snowing something fierce out there. The stranger won't be out on a night like this." People trusted Pastor Martin, and when he spoke they listened. "Tomorrow, I'll call Sheriff Kelley, and we'll see what he can do. Don't let this stranger ruin your Christmas."

He stopped talking when a man in a dark suit handed him a note. His eyes scanned the slip of paper, and he spoke again, "The way it looks now, I'm afraid we're going to have to cut our service short. The roads are getting bad out there." Sam looked and saw the snow piled high on the window sills. Truth be known, they were glad the service was over, because most of them didn't feel like celebrating. They just wanted to be safe at home behind locked doors.

To close the odd Christmas Eve service, Pastor Martin prayed for safety as they traveled home on the snowy roads and protection from the stranger. He finished with a solemn, "Amen," and then dismissed the congregation with a just-as-solemn "Merry Christmas everybody."

Sam and his folks gathered their coats, said Merry Christmas to a few friends, handed Mrs. Martin a plate of homemade cookies with sprinkles, and headed for their car. Pastor Martin was right. It was "snowing something fierce," and the snow was already over the tops of Sam's boots. Normally Sam would have loved to play in the deep snow, but the possibility of a run in with the stranger kept him from doing so.

On the drive home, Sam asked, "Dad, how come we're the only house the stranger hasn't stopped at?"

"I don't know, Sam," his dad answered. He didn't tell him he was wondering the same thing.

"You don't think he'd be out tonight, do you?" Sam asked.

"I think Pastor Martin is right," his dad answered. "It's snowing too hard outside. Besides, it's five below zero," he added, trying to reassure his son. "You don't have to worry. He won't be out on a night like this."

Sam hoped he was right, and so did his dad.

Inside the safety of their home, Sam forgot about the stranger and ran to the family room to plug in the Christmas tree. He knelt down between the tree and the wall, as he had every day for the last three weeks, and plugged in the lights. Nothing happened.

"Daaaddd, something's wrong with the Christmas tree lights," Sam yelled, hoping his dad was close by. "They won't turn on."

His dad took a look, and after several attempts to fix the problem, gave up.

"I guess we're going to have to enjoy the tree without lights this year," he said.

"Auugghh...what kind of Christmas is it without lights on the tree?" Sam whined.

As he said that, his mischievous dog, Charlie, shot by with something sticking out of his slobbery mouth. Sam chased after him, cornered him, and removed three mangled pieces taken from their nativity set. They were so chewed up that Sam had to look under the now dark tree where the nativity sat to see which figures had been eaten. To his horror, he found it was Mary, Joseph, and baby Jesus.

"Mommmmmm....Charlie chewed up Mary, Joseph, and Baby Jesus," he shouted.

His mother looked at the mangled plastic figures in his hand and tried to comfort her son. For Sam, this looked to be the worst Christmas ever.

Because it was a Christmas Eve tradition, Sam's dad started a fire in the fireplace, dimmed the lights, and turned on soft Christmas music. Outside, the wind howled and slapped at the house, making them feel snug and safe inside.

Although still upset about the ruined nativity figures and dark Christmas tree, Sam was just beginning to enjoy the music and fire, when all of a sudden, the music stopped, and the lights in the house went dark.

"Www...what happened?" Sam questioned, as fear and coldness crept over him.

"The storm probably knocked down a power line," his dad reassured him.

"It will be back on soon," his mom hoped out loud.

"Well, at least we have a nice fire and plenty of hot chocolate," his dad said. "You can bet we'll never forget this Christmas Eve."

Sam's dad had no idea how right he would be.

For the next hour, no one said much. They sat snuggled in a pile of blankets and listened to the wind whistle across the top of the chimney, hoping that the lights would come back on soon.

Then it happened.

Knock knock knock. They froze, hoping they hadn't heard the sound they feared might come. They held their breaths and listened.

Knock knock knock. A tingle ran down each of their backs.

Sam and his mother looked at his dad to see what he would do. He got up and headed for the door. Afraid to be left alone, Sam and his mother followed. His dad held a candle that cast long shadows around the dark rooms, and together they made their way to the front door when the knock came again. *Knock knock knock.* As they stopped and peered out the door, they saw a single dark figure standing in the swirling snow. In their hearts, they knew it was HIM.

Sam's mom started to say something, but her husband answered before she had even asked the question. "I can't leave him out in the cold and snow," he whispered loudly. "Don't worry, it'll be OK."

His dad reached out his hand, turned the knob, and woooooshhhh...the cold wind pushed the door open and snow spilled in through the crack. There, in the howling wind and knee-deep snow, stood the stranger.

He looked at Sam and his parents, and they looked at him. With a voice warm against the cold air, he said, "It's awfully cold out here. Would it be alright if I came in for a while?"

His dad hesitated just a second and then answered the shivering man, "Come on in."

"Thank you," he said with a look of surprise on his face. The stranger stomped the snow from his shoes, walked in, and Sam's dad ushered him into the room where they had been sitting.

"Here, sit down by the fire and warm up. Our power is off, so this is the best place in the house."

The stranger was tall and thin, and several of his yellow and brown teeth were missing. His hair and bushy beard were greasy and covered with snow that had begun to melt. He was

beyond dirty and smelled terrible. His only protection against the bitter cold was a filthy blanket wrapped around his shoulders.

Sam's mom brought the man a steaming cup of hot chocolate, and his dad handed him a thick, woolly blanket.

"This might help," he said, placing it over his shoulders.

"Thank you," the man whispered.

Sam's dad introduced himself and his family to the stranger and then asked their unexpected guest his name.

"Jesse," the man said softly. "My name is Jesse." He cupped the hot chocolate in his worn and dirty hands and relaxed his shoulders. The firelight shone bright in Jesse's eyes. Sam thought Jesse seemed overwhelmed by his family's kindness because he kept swallowing, like he was trying hard to hold back his emotions.

His mom and dad asked Jesse lots of questions, which he answered with short, simple answers. He wasn't trying to hide anything; he just didn't use a lot of words.

"You haven't gotten a very warm welcome around here," his dad finally said.

"Yeah, that's how it is most places I go," Jesse answered. Sam never saw anyone look as sad as Jesse did at that moment.

That night Jesse didn't say a whole lot. He mostly drank hot chocolate, smiled, and listened. Sam told him about the Christmas tree lights and the nativity figures, and Jesse laughed out loud when he described pulling them from his dog's slobbery mouth (which revealed that he had even less teeth than Sam first thought).

Jesse asked to see the mangled pieces so Sam disappeared into the dark part of the house and brought back the chewed pieces of plastic. Jesse smiled at the

teeth marks, set the pieces aside, leaned back, and pulled an ancient-looking knife from his pocket.

Sam's mom would have been startled had she seen the stranger holding the knife, but luckily she was in the kitchen getting more hot chocolate. When she returned, Jesse had chosen a small piece of wood stacked near the fireplace and was cutting large strips of bark from the stick.

A few minutes later, a figure of a man began to emerge from the stick. His hands worked quickly. Turning the stick, he cut deep gouges into the wood, and chips of wood piled up in Jesse's lap.

"You're very talented, Jesse," Sam's dad said with admiration.

Jesse smiled modestly, embarrassed by the attention.

"Who taught you how to carve like that?" Sam asked.

"My dad did," he answered thoughtfully.

They watched and asked questions occasionally while Jesse whittled. One hour turned into two, and then three, and the talking melted away until Sam and his family fell asleep as Jesse worked. It was quiet except for an occasional pop from the fire and the howling wind. The amazing thing was that Sam's family was able to sleep, even with the much talked about stranger sitting there. Perhaps it was because of the warmth of the room, for

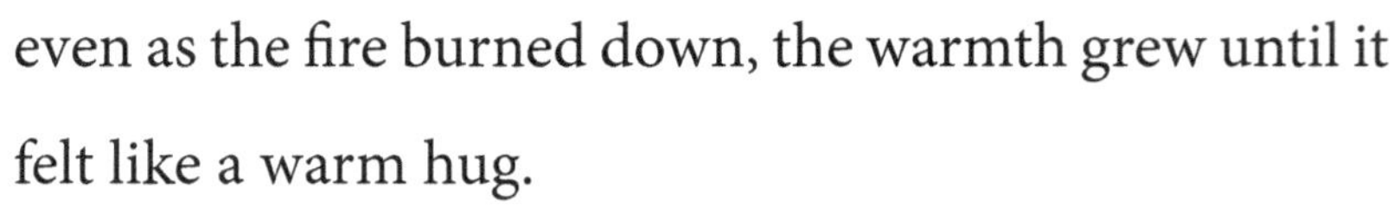

even as the fire burned down, the warmth grew until it felt like a warm hug.

At some point during the dark night, Sam awakened from his sound sleep. He opened his eyes and saw Jesse, with his blanket pulled up around his shoulders,

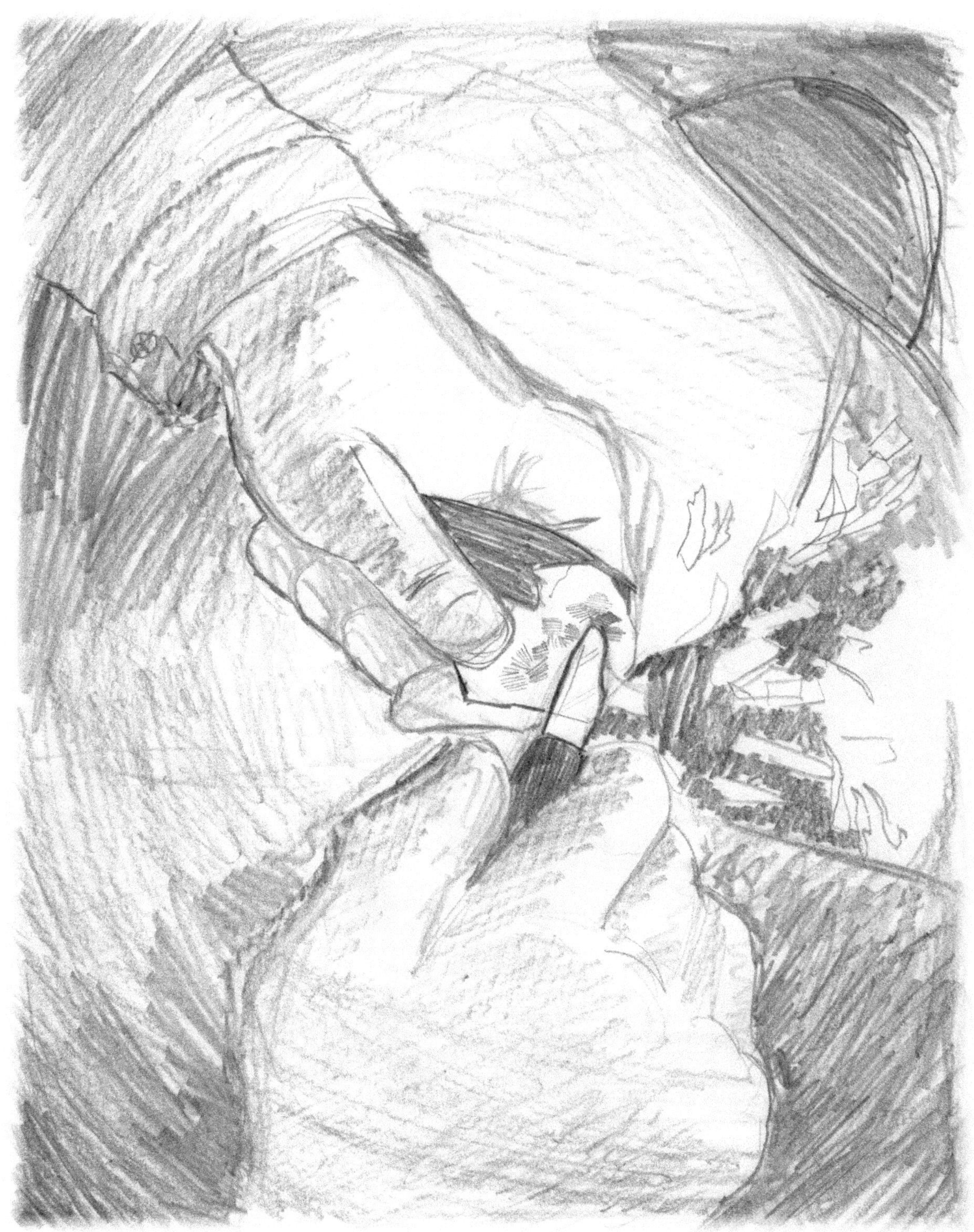

staring into the darkened fireplace. There wasn't much left of the fire except a few red coals and a pile of ashes, but the light of a blazing fire shone on Jesse's face.

It felt like a dream, but Sam knew he wasn't dreaming. Jesse's lips moved like he was singing, or praying, or maybe talking to himself or someone else, but no one else was awake in the room.

Sam watched for a while and saw a shiny tear make a path down Jesse's dirty cheek.

"Why is he crying?" Sam wondered. He couldn't decide if it was because his family had taken him in or because he was treated so badly by those in his church?

Sam was about to ask when Jesse slowly turned his face toward him. He thought about closing his eyes, pretending to be asleep, but for some reason he couldn't. Jesse looked at Sam, and Sam saw that Jesse's eyes flickered like the candles at the Christmas Eve service. Had it not felt so dreamlike, Sam might have screamed or burst out giggling.

"Thank you, Sam," he said softly. "Merry Christmas."

Sam smiled, but answering, "You're welcome" didn't seem like the right thing to say. Instead, he closed his eyes and was carried away by the warmth.

Early the next morning, Sam was awakened by a change that had taken place in the room. Christmas carols played softly on the radio, and the lights were shining on the Christmas tree. The power was back on and Christmas had come.

"Where is Jesse?" his mom asked.

For a minute, Sam had forgotten about the night before, but then he remembered. He turned and saw only the thick blanket that was gathered around the spot where Jesse sat. There was an empty cup, some wood shavings, and Jesse's dirty blanket, but there was no Jesse.

"I guess he had to leave," his dad said, tossing another log on the fire.

Sam got up and ran to the front door hoping that Jesse hadn't gotten far. Maybe he could invite him back for breakfast. When he got there, the snow was piled high against the door. The road that ran past their house was buried, and every tree was heavy with snow. In the whiteness, Sam was surprised that there were no tracks leading from their house. "The blowing snow couldn't have covered his tracks that fast," he thought. "Besides, he forgot his blanket."

Disappointed, Sam returned to the Christmas tree where his parents had placed all kinds of packages under it. He dropped to his knees to examine the gift tags, when something under the tree caught his eye. He looked closer and saw that Jesse had completed the missing pieces of the nativity set.

Although unpainted, they looked incredibly life-like. Sam lifted Joseph to his face. His forehead was wrinkled with worry and concern. Sam touched his tiny rugged hands and half expected the fingers to twitch. Mary looked so young and frail that Sam was afraid he'd hurt her if he held her too tight. After examining them closely, he picked up the smallest figure from the center of the nativity set.

It was Jesus, but he didn't look like any other baby Jesus Sam had ever seen. The baby wasn't smiling and didn't have chubby arms or hair of gold. This Jesus in the manger looked plain and...dirty.

As he held the tiny piece in his hand, the same strange warmth from the night before again wrapped itself around him. Sam smiled, placed the child back where He belonged, and ran to give his mom and dad a big hug. Christmas had come to his house.

That was the last time anyone ever saw the stranger. He just disappeared after that snowy Christmas Eve, and life returned to normal for the little church on the edge of town. But one nine-year-old boy and his family never forgot that night of the big snow and the visit from the stranger.

The End

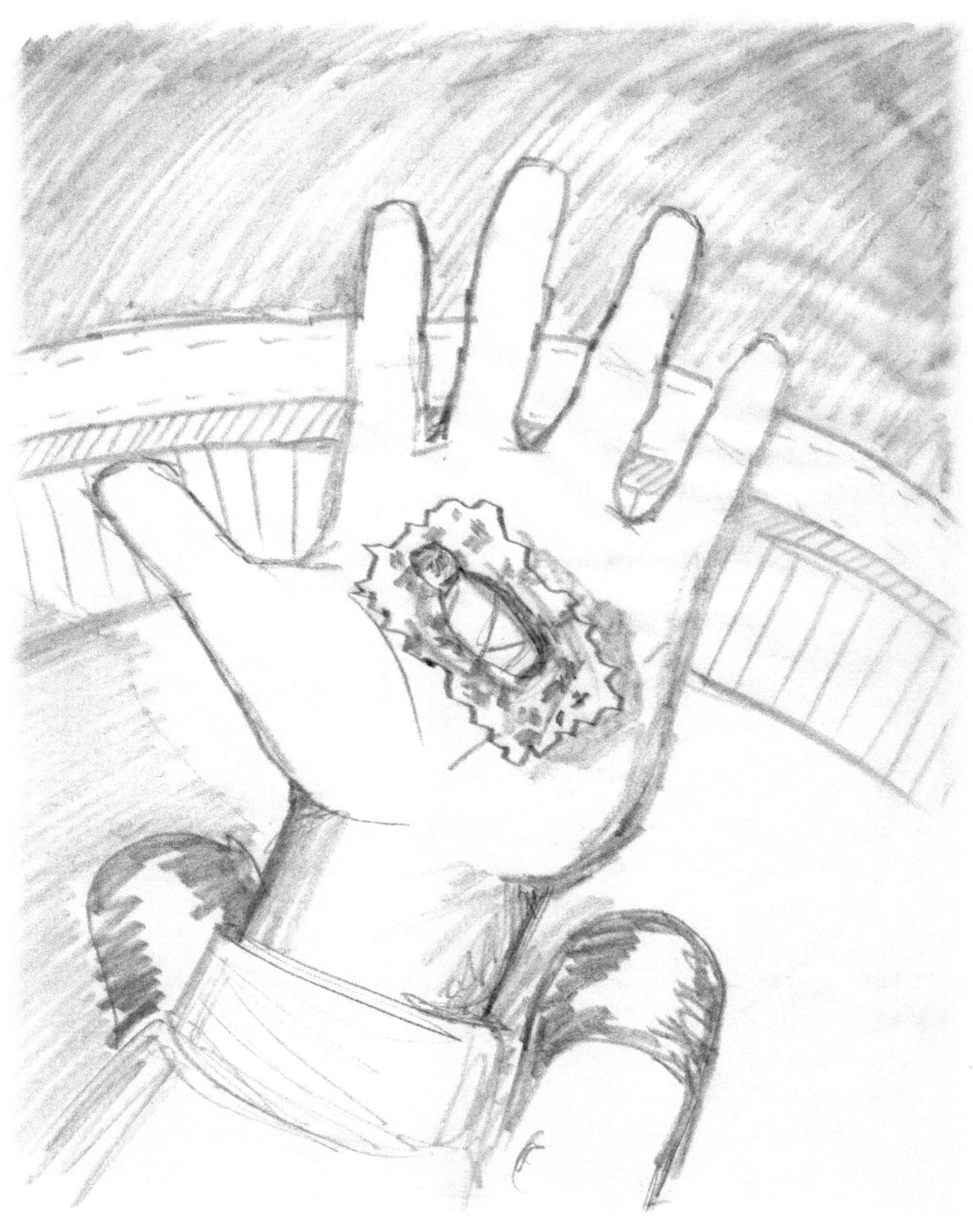

Epilogue

When the Son of Man comes in his glory, and all the angels with him, he will sit on his throne in heavenly glory. All the nations will be gathered before him, and he will separate the people one from another as a shepherd separates the sheep from the goats. He will put the sheep on his right and the goats on his left.

Then the King will say to those on his right, 'Come, you who are blessed by my Father; take your inheritance, the kingdom prepared for you since the creation of the world. For I was hungry and you gave me something to eat, I was thirsty and you gave me something to drink. I was a stranger and you invited me in, I needed clothes and you clothed me, I was sick and you looked after me, I was in prison and you came to visit me.'

Then the righteous will answer him, 'Lord, when did we see you hungry and feed you, or thirsty and give you something to drink? When did we see you a stranger and invite you in, or needing clothes and clothe you? When did we see you sick or in prison and go to visit you?'

The King will reply, 'I tell you the truth, whatever you did for one of the least of these brothers of mine, you did for me.

~Matthew 25:31-40

The Bishop's DREAM

Book Four
of
The Familyman's Christmas Treasury

written by
TODD WILSON

illustrated by SAM WILSON

Once upon a time, in the ancient town of Myra, there lived a simple man named Nicholas, Bishop Nicholas to be exact. Nicholas was old and wrinkled but loved God as much as any man could. It was his great love for God that made him the leader of a small group of Christians that met in Alexander the baker's home.

Unfortunately, little else is known of the Bishop except that he cared for the poor when others didn't. Many people of Myra lived in places where filth and debris filled the streets, and their homes were even worse. But Nicholas knew something that most people don't, and that is that helping others brings joy not only to oneself, but more importantly to God.

On his frequent trips to help those in need, word spread quickly that Nicholas was on his way. He was the one spark of light in their dark world, and the mere mention of his name gave people hope. He always arrived whistling like a bird and pulling his wobbly donkey named Jonathan behind him. It gave him great joy to see dozens of dirty children clothed in rags running towards him as fast as their skinny legs could carry them.

The children shouted as they drew closer and covered him with hugs and kisses. They loved Bishop Nicholas, not only for the food and clothing he brought, but also for caring about them, for giving them hope, and for telling them stories. For after everything in the pack on Jonathan's back was handed out, Nicholas led his donkey to a shady spot, gave him a cool drink of water, and sat down to tell them about the Carpenter who healed the lame, gave sight to the blind, and raised the dead.

Waving his hands through the hot, humid air, he described in great detail the life of God's Son. One moment, with excitement in his voice, Nicholas told how much the common people loved Jesus, and the next moment, while shaking his fist in anger, he spoke of the jealousy and hatred the religious leaders had for the Savior.

"Hoping to eliminate him, they plotted to kill him," he whispered. "Then one night, with the sky as dark as soot, they captured him, beat him, and crucified him." He paused as his lip quivered with emotion and then continued. "The cowards used the Romans to carry out their unthinkable plan, watched as soldiers nailed him to a cross, and then laughed as he slowly died," he said as tears streamed down his cheeks. The children wondered how Nicholas could love someone so much whom he had never even met.

With his head lowered, Nicholas continued, "They thought they had won." Then he sniffed away his tears, wiped his eyes with a tattered sleeve,

and lifted his head. His eyes twinkled and a smile grew on his face as he proclaimed, "But they were wrong." His audience clapped their hands and cheered wildly as he told the rest and best part of the story. "It was all part of God's plan to save the world," he quickly added. Nicholas looked into the dirty faces that society hated, and love filled his heart. He assured his listeners that Jesus loved them more than they could possibly imagine and hoping to prove this, he scooped a child up in his arms and hugged him with all his might.

Bishop Nicholas continued to laugh, hug, and talk until the sun dropped below the roof tops, casting long shadows on the dirty street. Then he announced to the children, "It's time for me to go because my journey isn't safe if it gets too late." "Besides," he added with a wink, "Jonathan is up past his bedtime." In disappointment, the children moaned and threw their arms around him, promising to let go only if he promised to come back soon.

Nicholas laughed a wonderful laugh and only half-heartedly struggled to free himself, while his dirty, young friends tightened their grasp and repeated their demand. Tiring, Bishop Nicholas agreed, as he always did, and together they fell in a heap on the dusty road. Brushing himself off, Nicholas stood, gathered his empty sacks, and tossed them on Jonathan's back for the long trip home. Like a parade, the children escorted him as far as they could and waved good-bye as he led his donkey out of sight.

On the trip home, the clip-clop of Jonathan's hooves was all that could be heard. Nicholas broke through the repetitious sound by singing a simple

song of praise to the One he loved, asking God to pour out His love on those the world ignored. With an indescribable joy in his heart, the tiredness of the day soon caught up with him and the little house that came into view was a welcome sight to his tired eyes.

Passing the front door, Nicholas led Jonathan around to his stall behind the little house, removed the empty bags from the donkey's back, patted him on the head, and checked the feed trough to make sure their was plenty for his trusted friend. As was his usual habit, he thanked Jonathan for his faithful service and wearily walked inside the tiny house.

Only a few pieces of furniture stood in the poorly lit room. A small fireplace nestled itself in one corner and a well-worn bed lay in another, but what caught the attention of everyone who visited Nicholas was the number of books scattered about. There were books covering the table, next to and under the bed, and stacked on the floor. Collected over a lifetime and filled with the teachings of Jesus and the church fathers, each was a treasure to be carefully guarded. Late into the night, Nicholas sat by the fire reading, spending most of his time studying his handwritten copy of the Holy Scriptures.

It was on that night, after having stoked the small fire and eaten a stale piece of bread that Nicholas plopped himself down in an old chair to read this tattered book. Exhausted and somewhat feverish after a day of giving, the Bishop slipped into a deep, deep sleep.

This was no ordinary sleep, however, for as he slept, a cold wind blew under the door sending a shower of sparks up the little chimney. As his sleep deepened, he drifted away to a far off dream that grew with brightness and

intensity until it was a dazzling blur of light. It was like looking at a field of flowers and seeing only an ocean of color. Ever so slowly, the heavenly vision focused until Nicholas found himself standing on a snow-covered street as people walked past him in all directions.

Snow floated softly from the sky like a million feathers, as a winter wind brushed his face, and a chill ran down his back. He had seen snow only twice in his many years so Nicholas enjoyed shuffling through it like a child enjoys a brand new toy. He looked up at the tall, dark buildings towering above and was startled by chariots without horses racing by him on the streets. Enchanting music seemingly coming out of nowhere added to the mystery of the place. While trying to wipe the dream from his eyes, Nicholas saw people bundled against the cold. They greeted one another in excited voices and many carried large boxes wrapped in shiny paper. It was more beautiful than anything Nicholas had ever imagined.

As if moved by an unseen hand, Nicholas started walking down the street, unaware of the strange way people were dressed. Oddly enough, everyone seemed blind to the fact that Nicholas looked so out of place. Instead, they turned to him and smiled, almost as if they recognized him so Nicholas smiled back. Everywhere he looked there were twinkling lights, evergreens covered with bright, shiny balls, and piles of snow. Nicholas knew something special was happening; he could feel it in the air, and he wondered why he had been brought there.

Although the language being spoken was new to him, Nicholas had no problem understanding the signs that filled the windows of the tall build-

ings. Bishop Nicholas saw a large sign that read 'SALE! Everything Half Off.' It made little sense to him until he saw a word he understood, *Christmas*. He had never heard of 'Christmas', but he recognized the words 'Christ' and 'Mass', which was the Latin word for ritual. So…this word *Christmas* must have something to do with the Savior, he thought. Pleased with his discovery, he walked in and out of the buildings, hoping to find the celebration honoring his Savior but instead found nothing.

What puzzled him most were the many drawings he saw of a heavy-set man with a long, white beard wearing beautiful red clothes. To make matters even more confusing, the strange man was surrounded by goat-like animals that had large horns coming from the tops of their heads. The man in red was dressed differently than everyone else in his dream, although Nicholas, like anyone who is dreaming, wasn't aware that it was a dream. He decided to find this man in the red suit and entered one of the buildings that displayed a large picture of him near its entrance.

Nicholas pushed through the revolving door and marveled at the way it moved. He would have loved to examine it more closely, but because of the urgency of his quest to find the man in the red suit, he continued on. The Bishop assumed he had entered some kind of indoor marketplace. It was filled with exotic clothing, colorful toys, and more people than he had ever seen. With wide eyes, Nicholas made his way through the crowded aisles, eventually coming to an open area where, to his surprise, he found the man in the red suit.

He was smaller than he expected and was sitting on a large, green chair next to a small house made of brightly colored food. Standing on either side of him were two young girls wearing pointy-toed shoes and a long line of children waiting to meet him. One by one the children were lifted onto his lap while the pointy-toed girl aimed a little black box toward them as they smiled and said, "Cheese". A bright light flashed and the parents of each child smiled warmly as though something wonderful had just taken place. Afterwards, the child and the man spoke for a few minutes and then one of the girls helped the child down as the next child in line mounted his big red lap, repeating the whole process.

Before long, Nicholas found himself also smiling as the event took place time after time and chuckled out loud as one of the little boys tugged on the man's white beard. A moment later, Bishop Nicholas noticed a sign in bright green letters that read *Have your picture taken with Santa Claus—$6.00*. He had no idea what $6 was but assumed that the man with the white beard must be Santa Claus. The name meant nothing to him and after having stood for quite some time, Nicholas knew he must leave.

Nicholas wandered back through the store searching for the revolving door through which he had entered. He was starting to piece together that Santa Claus must have something to do with Christmas but he wasn't sure why. Suddenly, he spun back through the door and found himself standing outside in the falling snow again. The cool air felt good on his flushed face, and Nicholas was glad to be out of the crowded building.

Not knowing where to go next, he stopped dead in his tracks, as if waiting for someone to point the way, when he was swept up into a group of people rushing down the sidewalk. The people surrounding him smiled and laughed as though they were under a delightful spell, but the spirit of what was happening in this strange place skipped over Nicholas. In fact, the farther he went, the more perplexed he became until his gaze landed on a large shadow in front of his feet, and the crowd around him vanished.

Lifting his head, Nicholas saw a word he recognized for sure. A big sign read, *Bedford Community Church*. What Bedford Community meant he wasn't sure, but the word 'church' was plain to him. This was a place where Christians gathered to worship Jesus. In all his travels he had never seen a church that met in such a large building, but he felt certain that someone would be in it that could help him understand what Christmas and Santa Claus were all about.

Nicholas opened the heavy door of the large stone building and walked into a room filled with long benches. Looking towards the front of the room, his eyes rested on a plain, simple cross that hung on the wall. Pain mixed with triumph filled his heart since many of his friends had been put to death on such a cross, including the Lord Himself when he was crucified for the sins of the world. Nicholas stood there staring at the cross when a friendly voice behind him said, "May I help you?" Forgetting any pleasantries, Nicholas abruptly asked, "Can you tell me about Christmas?"

Almost as if expecting Nicholas to ask that question, the pastor answered, "Well, Christmas is the day we celebrate the birth of Christ." Nicholas had

Bedford
Community Church

been in the habit of celebrating the resurrection, as had the entire church of his time, but he had never celebrated Jesus' birth before. After briefly mulling it over in his mind, he decided it would be a good thing to do and hoped he'd remember to do so when he returned home.

"But what about Santa Claus?" Nicholas asked. "Why does Santa Claus play such an important role in Christmas?" The young pastor motioned for Nicholas to join him as they made their way up front and sat in one of the empty benches near the cross on the wall.

"Well, Santa Claus is a fictional character," the pastor answered. "He lives at the North Pole, makes toys for all the boys and girls in the world, and then delivers them on Christmas Eve in a sleigh drawn by flying reindeer." The Bishop stared blankly at the pastor.

"But...what does Santa Claus have to do with Jesus?" he blurted out.

"Well, nothing. He just kind of took his place," the pastor responded, feeling embarrassed by his own admission of the truth.

"Why? How could this have happened?" Nicholas asked.

"Well," the pastor continued, "we get the tradition from the Dutch. A long time ago when they came to this country they brought with them the story of Santa Claus. He was generous and gave gifts to the children. We call him Santa Claus because it sounds like the name they gave him, "Sinter Claus," which meant Saint Nicholas." The Bishop was struck by the similarity to his own name but knew he was no more a saint than all Christians were.

"Well, where do they say this Saint Nicholas came from?" the Bishop questioned.

"Tradition has it that he performed miracles and brought three murdered children back to life..." the pastor answered. The Bishop was deep in thought as the pastor spoke. Nicholas knew this wasn't possible, because not since the Lord's apostles had such miracles taken place, but not wanting to interrupt the pastor, he listened on. "They say that he was a Bishop in Myra in 325 AD." As the pastor spoke those words, a chill blew through the Bishop's soul like a candle being snuffed out.

Nicholas felt a sickening numbness spread across his body, and after a moment, he whispered in the saddest voice ever spoken, "..............*but Christmas is about Him, not me.*"

The Pastor, who looked as though he knew all along who he was talking to, reached over and placed a hand on the Bishop's shoulder and said understandingly as he stood to leave, "I know." And then he was gone.

Nicholas sat there unable to move. How had it happened? How could people have placed him above his Savior, the one whom he had served for so many years? Nicholas sat looking at the cross in disbelief and then slowly stood to go. As he turned to leave, he noticed a soft glow radiating from the back of the church. Nicholas made his way to the source of the glow and found miniature plastic figures at the base of a lighted evergreen tree. Nestled amongst the plastic cows, sheep, and donkey was a manger filled with fresh straw holding a baby.

Nicholas' eyes filled with tears as he stared at the Christ child, and then he reverently knelt before the little one in the manger. He bowed his head, closed his eyes, and cried, "It's about you, not me."

With tears streaming down his wrinkled face, he opened his eyes and found himself back in his home and sitting in his chair, as the book in his hand fell to the floor with a soft thump. It had all been a dream, a very real dream. Nicholas looked around, thankful to be home and slowly pulled himself from his chair. Although feeling exhausted from the day's activities, he knelt in front of the fireplace that held a few dying embers. With closed eyes, he whispered this simple prayer: *It's all about you, not me.* Then, picturing the children on the fat man's lap, he smiled and added, "Help them to remember that."

The End

Harold Grubbs

and the
Christmas Vest

Book Five
of
The Familyman's Christmas Treasury

written and illustrated by

TODD WILSON

For Isaac's dad, the first Sunday morning after Thanksgiving was very special. Each year on this day, he reached deep into the back of his crowded closet and fished around for something that had been buried in a mound of clothes for eleven months. His fingers poked and prodded through corduroy pants, wool sweaters, and scratchy jackets. Then he touched something soft and worn. He had found it.

With a smile of satisfaction, he extracted a festive red Christmas-plaid vest that looked more like a Christmas tablecloth than something to wear.

His eyes lit up as he removed the vest from its special golden hanger. Carefully, he slid one arm in, then the other, and buttoned the shiny brass buttons up the front. He took two steps back, looked in the mirror that hung on a wall, stuck his thumb and forefinger in both of the tiny pockets on the vest, and proudly examined his outfit.

Just then Isaac glanced in the open doorway and asked, "Dad, are you going to wear that vest again this year?"

"Of course I am," he said in astonishment. "This is my Christmas vest, and today is the first Sunday after Thanksgiving" he added, as if everyone should know what that meant.

"But nobody else's dad wears a Christmas vest," Isaac argued.

"That's exactly why I need to wear it," his Dad responded. "Everyone is counting on me."

Isaac knew that was true, and if he had to be honest, he really kind of liked it. "Dad, how long have you had that old vest?"

His dad paused, pondering the question. "Well, I got it way before you were born."

"Where did you get it?" Isaac asked.

His dad beamed a big smile, and Isaac knew a story was about to be told. His dad loved to tell stories, and Isaac loved to hear them.

"I wasn't the first owner of this Christmas vest, you know?" his dad said.

"You weren't?" Isaac asked. "Who had it before you?"

"A man by the name of Harold Grubbs." The edges of his dad's mouth curled up in a funny way when he said his name. "He lived uptown from where your Granddad and Grammy live. When I was a kid, he was about the meanest man in town, and he liked it that way.

I'm not sure why he was so mean, but Granddad told me that his wife

was killed in a fire, and he just never got over it. He never remarried and never had children. So…whatever the reason, he hated children, and I was scared of him."

Isaac's mouth hung open as he listened.

"But then something happened," his dad said. "I guess I must have been about your age at the time. Mr. Grubbs showed up at church one Sunday. He had never gone before in his whole life, but on that day, he walked in dressed in a suit that looked three sizes too small.

Everyone noticed and stared. He had the saddest, most miserable look on his face. He sat near the back, listened to the whole service, and then got up and left without saying a word to anyone."

"Well, then what happened?" Isaac interrupted.

"Nothing, that Sunday," his dad answered. "He came back the next several Sundays looking just as miserable. He came in, sat in the same seat, listened carefully, and then got up and left."

"He never talked to anyone?" Isaac asked.

"Never. Then one Sunday, he looked different. He wore the same misfit suit, but his face seemed softer. He even said good morning to someone near the front door."

Isaac smiled as his dad went on. The story was getting good.

"Mr. Grubbs took his seat and listened carefully like always. Then, as we were singing the last song, he stepped from his pew and made his way up front. You should have been there. The singing almost stopped because

everyone was so busy looking at Mr. Grubbs. Mrs. Bee, the church organ-ist, nearly fell off her bench."

Isaac giggled at the picture in his mind.

"But, Mr. Grubbs didn't seem to notice at all. He walked straight up to the pastor, who was just as surprised as everyone else. They talked for a minute, and then pastor put his arm around Mr. Grubbs's shoulder. It was the first time in a long time that anyone had touched him. Mr. Grubbs was smiling, and I saw tears running down his cheeks. At the end of the song, we sat down, and the pastor said Mr. Grubbs had given his heart to Jesus."

"Everyone was stunned. I guess they assumed he was too hardened for God to break through, but as it slowly sank in, they smiled and several whispered, Amen. After the service, people went up to shake his hand and talk with him."

Isaac's dad's eyes glistened with tears.

"That Sunday was the Sunday before Thanksgiving. The next Sunday, Mr. Grubbs walked into church wearing a bright red Christmas plaid vest under his old suit. It was just like Ebenezer Scrooge after his visit from the ghosts. He smiled and greeted everybody he saw. It was all I could do to keep from staring. I couldn't believe this was the same mean Mr. Grubbs I had known my whole life, and from the looks on everyone's faces, no one else could believe it either."

Isaac smiled and pointed to his father's vest. "And that's his vest right?"

"Now don't get ahead of me, Isaac...When Mr. Grubbs took his seat that

Sunday, he sang louder than six people. But the thing I remember most was the way he stood while he sang. He held the hymnal in one hand, and put the thumb and forefinger of his other hand in the little pocket of his Christmas vest. While he stood there singing, he rubbed his fingers together inside the pocket.

"Why do you think he did that?" Isaac asked.

"Just wait. We'll get to that part," his dad answered. "Jesus had changed Mr. Grubbs. He was never the same again.

He went from being the meanest man in town to the nicest. He especially loved the kids. He tickled us, talked to us, and brought us little treats. There was hardly a time that he didn't have a smile on his face or candy in his pocket."

His dad paused briefly as he stared out the window and then continued. "What I remember most was that he never quit talking about what God had done in his life. And when he did, his eyes got all wet with tears."

"Every Sunday through December he wore that vest, and whenever he stood, he had his fingers in his vest pockets. It was that way for years. People kind of counted on him to wear that vest. It became part of Christmas for a lot of people - including me."

"Then what happened?"

"Well, I went away to college. Mr. Grubbs got real sick that year and died a few weeks before Christmas. I wasn't able to go to the funeral, but I was told that it was the happiest funeral people had ever been to."

"Yeah, but how did you get his vest?" Isaac asked. "I mean this is his vest, right?"

"Just wait...I'm getting to that part," his dad said chuckling. "Anyway, I came home from college a couple weeks later, and there was an estate sale to get rid of Mr. Grubbs's belongings. It was a snowy day, and Granddad, Grammy, and I went.

It was freezing cold and not many people turned out for the sale. I guess he really didn't have anything of much value, just a bunch of worn out furniture and some knick knacks. We looked through some boxes of junk and were about to leave when I saw a rack of old clothes and...his Christmas vest.

Sure enough, it was the Christmas vest we had all grown to love. I was surprised by how nice it seemed among the rest of the old clothing. He had taken special care of it, even hanging it on an elaborate golden hanger."

Isaac eyed the hanger in his hands. It was painted gold and a little manger had been carved in its center.

"My parents laughed when I bought it and teased me about how nice it would look at college.

"I packed the vest away, because Granddad was right, I wasn't going to wear it at college.

That's where I met your Mom though, and a few years later we got married. Three or four years after that, I found the Christmas vest packed in a box of ornaments in the basement. Seeing it, was like seeing Mr. Grubbs all

over again...not the mean Mr. Grubbs but the changed one."

"You should have heard the teasing I got when I stepped into the church building on that first Sunday after Thanksgiving. I wanted to hide, but you just can't hide this vest. I decided that wearing it maybe wasn't such a good idea after all. When we got home from church, I was about to take it off and pack it away forever when I caught a glimpse of myself in the mirror."

"As I stood there, my hands made their way to the little pockets on the vest, and just like Mr. Grubbs, I placed my thumb and forefinger in the pockets. When I did, I was surprised to feel something in each pocket.

In one pocket, I found a big old nail that had been polished smooth by years of rubbing. In the other pocket, there was a straw mat about the size of a playing card. Like the nail, it had been rubbed until it was ragged. As I held the nail and the straw mat, I knew now why Mr. Grubbs had kept his fingers in his vest pockets every time he wore the vest. It reminded him that the child who had been born in a manger had also been nailed to a cross. More importantly, Jesus had been crucified for him, a mean old man who hated everyone."

Isaac's dad took a deep breath. "So, ever since that Sunday morning years ago, I've worn this vest from the first Sunday after Thanksgiving all the way through Christmas. It reminds me that Jesus still changes people."

"Now let's get going or we'll be late for church," his dad said.

Isaac was about to leave when he turned back to his dad and asked, "Dad, what did you do with the old nail and the straw mat?"

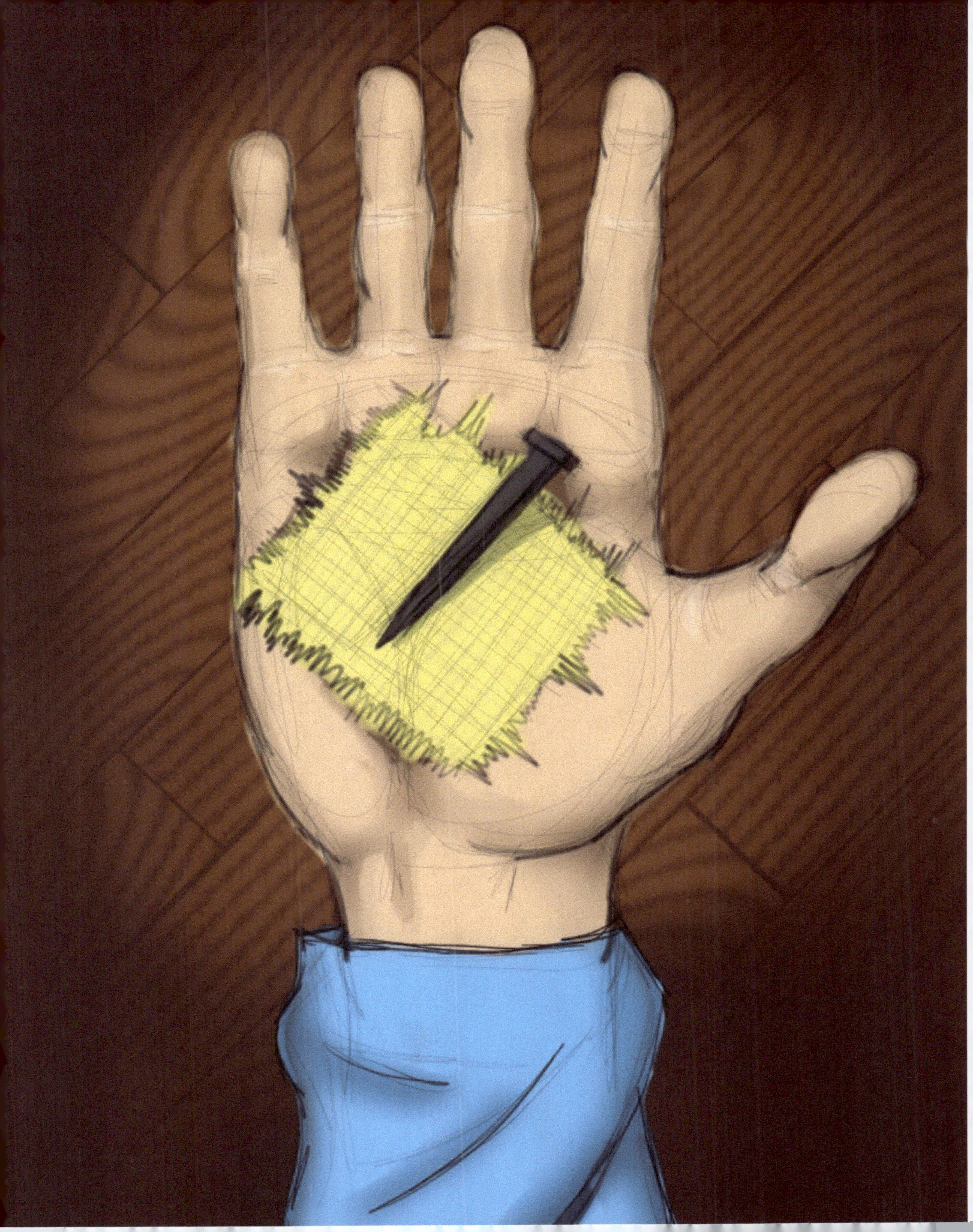

His dad, who was fixing his tie in the mirror, stopped and turned to Isaac. He looked at his son, stuck his thumb and forefinger into his vest pockets, and pulled from one pocket, a well worn nail, and a ragged straw mat from the other. He held them for his son to examine and touch.

"I keep them right in here so I won't forget," his dad said with a smile. "Mr. Grubbs would like that."

The End

Gladys Remembers Christmas

Book Six
of
The Familyman's Christmas Treasury

written by
TODD WILSON

illustrated by SAM WILSON

$\mathcal{C}$an you imagine anyone NOT liking Christmas? Well, that's exactly how Gladys Higgins felt. She may not have hated the holiday as much as Ebenezer Scrooge did, but Gladys hated Christmas as much as she hated her name.

Gladys was named after her mother, who died when she was only six years old. Even as a child Gladys thought her name sounded so…plain and old fashioned. She tried shortening it to Glady, but that just made it worse. So she was stuck with plain ol' Gladys.

Her father, who never remarried, was a stern man, to say the least. Her older brothers said that he used to be fun before their mother died, but Gladys had a hard time believing that. It wasn't that her dad didn't try. He did. He made sure they were well-clothed and had three hot meals a day. In fact, they lacked nothing, except the one thing that Gladys wanted more than anything…to be loved (and to have a different name).

That's why Gladys hated Christmas, because it was a reminder that everyone else was happy, and she wasn't. As she got older, she often wished she could skip the whole month of December…along with all of its decorations, gift giving, and holiday cheer.

She found herself thinking those very thoughts one cold December morning. You see, Gladys had taken the day off from work to clean out her father's house. He was ninety-years-old, and she had moved him into a nursing home the week before.

Her brothers were scattered across the country with families of their own, so Gladys was left with deciding what to keep and what to sell. She dreaded the thought of wading through sixty years of junk, but she was not one to put things off. If she had learned anything in her hard life, it was to face problems head on.

Gladys was up extra early that day, with a cup of coffee and the morning paper. As usual, the radio was on to drown out the silence. She gradually noticed a familiar Christmas tune drifting from the speakers. It was the first holiday song of the season. To anyone else it would have announced the beginning of Christmas, but to her it was as if someone was scraping fingernails across a chalkboard.

"I don't need THAT this morning," she said with her lips against the cup, and with a quick 'click,' it was off.

After finishing her coffee and paper in silence, Gladys tidied up the kitchen, grabbed her work clothes from the back of the closet, got dressed, and loaded her car with a broom, dustpan, vacuum cleaner, mop, and bucket. On the way to her father's house, she stopped at a store to pick up three boxes of heavy-duty trash

bags. For the rest of the drive, she wondered if three boxes would be enough.

Pulling up in front of the old house, she felt a twinge of nostalgia, which for her was as good as an avalanche of emotion. The house scared her as a child. It was big and drafty, and her father kept the house dark and cool to save on electricity. But now, a light dusting of snow actually made the old place look warm and inviting.

It was hard to believe that any fond memories could be coming from her old house. There were none from when she had lived there. She had no memory of the smell of cookies right out of the oven on a cold winter day or the taste of fresh lemonade on the front porch in the summer. Her father was too busy for that. If there were cookies, they were made by Gladys (and everyone knows that cookies you bake yourself never smell as good as ones baked by your mother).

It took a couple of trips up and down the front steps to get all her cleaning supplies inside, but after she had unloaded the car she was finally ready to tackle the project. Inside, the house smelled like her father...old and sad, like mothballs and hard work.

Gladys walked over to the thermostat and turned the knob to seventy-five, guessing it was the first time it had ever been above sixty. With a soft whoosh, the furnace kicked to life, and warm air gushed from the dusty registers in the floor.

The morning went by quickly. Gladys emptied the bathroom closet and medicine cabinet and cleaned under the sink. After that, she rummaged through the hall closet and then sorted some old papers that had been stuffed into a desk drawer.

After lunch, Gladys pulled all the dishes from the cabinets and packed them away in boxes to take home. She then spent the rest of the afternoon cleaning out the upstairs closets. By the end of the day she was exhausted, but she was determined to clean out the attic before going home.

As a girl, the attic had always seemed scary. Gladys had almost forgotten it was part of the house until her father asked her to find something in the attic and bring it to him at the nursing home. He didn't tell her what it was exactly, he just said it was in a green cardboard box…near some old Christmas ornaments.

The entrance to the attic was deep inside the closet of her father's bedroom. Gladys fumbled for the light and turned sideways to scoot towards the back of the closet where the attic door stood. By the time she finally opened the closet door, the sun had set, and the house felt cold, even with the furnace working overtime.

Gladys couldn't remember the last time she had climbed the attic stairs, but when she turned the knob and opened the door, the squeak sounded familiar. Amazingly, her hand found the attic light switch as easily as if she used the door a dozen times a week. Light bulbs sprang to life at the top of the worn, wooden stairs, casting a warm beam of light down the stairwell and into the closet.

Each step squeaked loudly and the thought of haunted houses filled Gladys' mind as she made her way up.

At the top of the landing, she looked around at the large, cluttered space.

The attic was just the kind you'd expect to find in a big, old house. Old, broken, and discarded things filled the musty space.

For the first time all day, Gladys felt overwhelmed by the amount of stuff to go through. Since there was no chance of getting through it all, she decided to look for the box her father wanted and call it a night.

Even that proved to be a bigger challenge than she expected.

"Near old Christmas ornaments," she repeated her father's directions to herself. "Oh, that helps a lot. There are old Christmas decorations everywhere!"

Every nook and cranny was filled with dusty, artificial garland, large outdoor yard ornaments, boxes of decorations in all sizes, and colored bulbs in neatly-wound bundles. This was a bigger surprise to Gladys than it would have been to you or me, because her family had barely even celebrated the holiday.

As far back as Gladys could remember they had never had a Christmas tree, decorations, or Christmas lights. She had never even made paper chains out of red and green construction paper to count down the days until Christmas. Christmas morning only consisted of a present or two sitting next to her spot at the kitchen table. She'd open her gifts, and that was the end of the celebration until the next year.

Now here she was, up to her elbows in Christmas decorations. She almost wondered if they belonged to the previous homeowners but decided that they had to be theirs. After rooting through half a dozen boxes of Christmas ornaments, Gladys finally found the green box.

It wasn't heavy, but the box felt flimsy, and she feared the bottom might give way. She scooted it out into the middle of the room where the light was brighter, but a strange, warm smell stopped her dead in her tracks.

Her first thought was that it might be an electrical short, and she half expected the attic to burst into flames at any moment. It didn't, but the smell grew stronger and warmer until Gladys was afraid to move. She tried to see, hear, and smell what was going on, all at the same time.

The longer she stood sniffing the air, the more certain she was that something was baking in the oven.

"Gladys!" a woman's voice called from somewhere downstairs.

Gladys nearly jumped out of her skin.

"Gladys, did you find it?" the voice asked, this time sounding closer.

"Yeah…I think so," she heard herself answer, as if in a dream.

The sound of footsteps echoed up the main stairs, down the hallway below, into her father's bedroom, and then into the closet! If the voice had not sounded so warm and non-threatening, Gladys would have been looking for a good hiding spot and something large and heavy to swing. Whoever was calling to her was now at the base of the attic stairs.

"Do you need some help with the box?" the voice asked knowingly.

"I guess," Gladys answered, "I'm afraid the bottom might fall out."

"I told your father we should have packed it away in a new box," the woman said climbing the stairs, "but he didn't want to because this is the box it came in… he's so sentimental."

The woman glanced at Gladys and walked straight towards her. "There you are," she said. "I was beginning to think you got lost up here."

Gladys couldn't believe her eyes. It was her mother! Just like she remembered her...or hadn't remembered her in such a long time.

"Can I help you carry the box?" she asked.

"Sure, uh...uh...that would be great...Mom."

That word sounded so good coming from her mouth...like saying the name of someone you haven't thought about in years. Her own voice sounded fresh and young...different, but the same.

"Your father will be so glad to see this set up," her mother said cheerfully.

Gladys just stared.

Together, they carefully carried the box down the attic steps. Gladys studied the face across from hers. She had forgotten how pretty her mother was and how good she smelled. Gladys just about dropped the box when they stepped out of the closet and into her father's room. The cold, drab room had vanished. Instead, she found the room exactly as she remembered it before her mother died.

A gold lamp with fringe around its shade stood next to the bed, throwing a welcoming light across the room. A bouquet of flowers sat on her mother's dresser. Gladys had forgotten how much her mother loved flowers. She had forgotten how safe and snug her parent's room felt and how she loved lying in bed with them on Saturday mornings.

On their way down to the main floor, she heard a scratchy Bing Crosby Christmas album playing on the large, console stereo in the corner.

"We gave that away years ago," Gladys thought.

Somehow, the house had come alive. Boxes of Christmas decorations littered the floor, and the furniture by the big picture window had been moved to make room for a Christmas tree. Suddenly, as if waking up from a dream, Gladys remembered.

"Let's set the box by the front window," her mother instructed. "I think it will look nice under the tree this year."

Gladys couldn't speak.

"I hope we can get it set up before your father gets home," she added with a twinkle in her eye.

"Oh, I forgot the cookies," she shouted. "They're probably burnt to a crisp!"

She raced to the kitchen, and Gladys heard her mother's heels click across the linoleum floor. That sound, along with the creak of the oven door and the scrape of the cookie tray across the rack released a flood of memories.

While her mother was checking on the cookies, Gladys sat on her knees, mesmerized by the transformation. Everything was exactly like she should have remembered it…the old couch with Grandma's afghan stretched across the back, the green recliner with white doilies over the armrests, and the braided rug in the dining room. Her eyes widened when she spied her favorite doll curled up on the couch.

"Janet," she gasped, "I forgot about you."

She scrambled to her feet, ran to the couch, and scooped Janet up, pulling her to her chest. Ahhh….she smelled just like she used to. How could she have forgotten all the tea parties and shared secrets? But, she had. She had forgotten…everything.

Her reunion was interrupted as her mother walked out of the kitchen carrying a plate of freshly baked, chocolate chip cookies. "Oh, you found Janet," she said. "I found her wedged between the couch and the wall this afternoon. I thought you'd be glad to see her."

Tears glistened in Gladys' eyes. She was overwhelmed by the doll, the house, and the chocolate chip cookies…but mostly by her mother…the way she walked, her voice, the crinkles around her eyes when she smiled…everything.

"Let's eat these cookies over by the front window and watch for your father," her mother said. Gladys eyed the large, slightly-burned, chocolate chip cookies. Nothing had ever looked or smelled so good. She picked up one and took a big bite. It tasted like home and Christmas.

"Come on, Gladys, let's get the set out now," her mother said.

Her mother set the plate on the coffee table and kneeled beside the box. With a cookie in one hand and crumbs around her mouth, Gladys watched as her mother pulled off the lid and removed some old, yellowed newspaper from the box. She had no idea what was inside.

Next, her mother pulled a tiny ceramic shepherd from the box and examined him to see how he had fared his season of storage. Now, Gladys remembered! It was the nativity set that her father had gotten her mother on their very first Christmas together. She remembered her father telling the story each year of how he had paid five dollars for the set and how that was a lot of money back then.

Her mother pulled piece after piece from the worn box, placing them beside the shepherd. With each one, Gladys remembered a little more. She remembered walking the wise men through the house, pretending they were on their journey, and her brothers dive-bombing the shepherds with the Angel of the Lord.

She watched as her mother set down a lamb and then snatched it back up and looked at the spot where a tail used to be.

"Every time I sweep, I think I'll find that sheep's tail," she said with a smile.

Gladys remembered breaking it off when she was five-years-old. She had dropped it when one of her older brothers came up behind her and scared her. Gladys put the sheep down and picked up another piece, then another. Her hands remembered each fold and crease of their ceramic clothing.

After each piece had been accounted for, her mother stuffed the newspaper back in the box and slid it out of the way.

"Now, we can set it up," she said with a smile.

First, there was the wooden stable. Her father had made it from an old apple crate. Once it was in place, Gladys helped arrange the nativity pieces inside it. The last piece, according to tradition, was the Baby in the manger. Her mother gave her the honor of placing it in the middle of the others.

Gladys dropped to her belly, forgetting that she had started the day off as a fifty-eight-year-old woman, and rested her chin on her folded hands to get as close as she could to the Christ Child.

A million forgotten feelings filled her heart. She remembered holding the

miniature Baby and pretending that she was Mary, staring at Him in the light of the Christmas tree, and listening to the story of His birth that her father told so many times during the month of December.

He quit telling that story after her mother died. A lump caught in Gladys' throat as she remembered their last Christmas together. Her mother was sick, and she was scared. It was Christmas Eve. She was having trouble sleeping so she got up, snuck downstairs to the nativity scene, and got on her belly, just as she was doing now.

The words she prayed that night flooded her mind, "Dear Jesus, please make my mom better…don't take her to heaven yet."

Within a month, her mother died, and she never saw the little Baby in the manger again. Christmas was packed away and stored in the attic…and forgotten.

Overwhelmed by emotion, Gladys whirled around and threw her arms around her mother's neck sobbing, "I've missed you so much, Mom…I love you…I love you so much!"

Her mother held her as tightly as only a mother can. "I know, Honey. I love you more than anything."

Both mother and child cried, but the tears felt good.

"But Gladys," her mother finally said, stroking her daughter's hair, "He loves you more, even more than I do."
"You mean Dad?" Gladys asked.

"Yes, your dad loves you, but someone else loves you even more." Her mother wiped the tears from her daughter's eyes and brushed a wisp of dark hair from her face.

"Who?" Gladys sniffed.

Her mother pointed to the little figure in the manger. "Him," she said, "Don't ever forget that, Gladys. No matter what."

Gladys turned to see the tiny figure. As careful as a little girl can be, she picked up the tiny Baby and held it in the palms of her hands, and then…Gladys remembered Christmas.

She remembered how much she was loved, by her mom and her dad, but most of all, by God.

"But Mom…" she started, but her mother was gone. Janet was gone and the smell of cookies, the decorations, and the music…were all gone.

Gladys sat, surrounded by the nativity figures, in front of the big, dark window. For the first time in a long time, Gladys felt loved. She sat and enjoyed the forgotten feeling for a long moment and then slowly packed the pieces back into the green box and shut the lid.

Stiffly, she stood and carried the box to the front door where her coat lay crumpled over her purse. As she bent over to get her coat, something in the crack between the floor-boards caught her eye. It looked like a tooth. Gladys did a quick sweep with her tongue to make sure none of her crowns were missing and was relieved to find all of her teeth in their proper place.

With little effort, she plucked the small white 'thing' from the crack and held it up to the light coming through the window to get a better look. Tears gathered in the corner of her eyes, and a lump crept into her throat. It was the tail to the

little lamb she had broken over fifty years ago. She swallowed hard, and tucked the little piece into her pocket to be re-attached later that night.

Slinging her purse over her shoulder, Gladys turned to give the house one last look. It wasn't the same house she had entered that morning. This house was filled with warmth and good memories…Christmas memories.

Gladys walked out into the frigid cold and locked the door behind her. She had one more stop to make before heading home. With the green box beside her, she drove to the nursing home to set up the ceramic figures and wooden stable for her father.

"He'll be so surprised," she could almost hear her mother say.

Her father was surprised. And on that cold December night, he and Gladys remembered together: her mother, Christmas, and the love of the Child born in the manger so many years before. And from that night on, Gladys not only loved Christmas more than most people did, she also loved her name.

The End

The Secret of the Snow Village

Book Seven

of

The Familyman's Christmas Treasury

written by

TODD WILSON

Photography by KAT WILSON

On Christmas Eve, the falling snow reminded everyone at Katherine's grandmother's house of a Christmas card. They had all gathered for their annual Christmas celebration, and like every Christmas Eve, something magical was about to happen.

After all, it was on that night long ago that angels announced the birth of God's Son. Songs have been written of its mystery, poems and stories as well, and on this particular night, many years ago, something happened to Katherine that she'll never forget.

Her grandmother's house was a lovely place at Christmas time. Decorations, ornaments, and memories cluttered the house, and a plump Christmas tree made the corner of the family room glow like a stained glass window. The highlight of her grandmother's decorating effort, however, was in the living room, where dozens of shiny, ceramic buildings were carefully set up into a quaint, Christmas village.

Nestled in a blanket of snowy cotton were houses decorated with wreaths and Christmas lights, old buildings with glowing windows on Main Street, a white church, a red barn, a restaurant, a movie theater, a carousel, and even a houseboat floating on a frozen pond made from aluminum foil. It took Katherine's grandmother several days to carefully unpack the pieces from their cardboard boxes and create the little village.

Among the glowing, magical buildings, there stood shiny, miniature people who appeared frozen in time. Children played in the streets, a man perched on a ladder decorated his house, and three kids dressed as a Christmas tree, a star, and

a Santa Claus, hurried to a Christmas pageant. Near a rustic hunting lodge, a family skated on the aluminum foil pond, and at the intersection of a busy, brick street, a policeman stood, stone still, directing traffic, while an old truck sat motionless, pushing a few balls of cotton.

Staring at the delightful Christmas town, Katherine spent most of the evening with her chin at street level imagining the story taking place in the snowy village. Her mother had to drag her away from the village when dinner was ready.

After dinner, while the others talked and played, Katherine slipped off to resume her spot in the now dark room. Dark, that is, except for the tiny lights that shone from the little buildings and homes nestled in the snow.

On any other Christmas Eve this would have been quite out of character for Katherine. Always right in the middle of everything, Katherine was known for being...well...busy. For most of November and all of December she had been enjoying Christmas.

She did the usual holiday activities: decorated the Christmas tree with home-made ornaments, made paper chains, listened to Christmas songs on the radio, and created an endless list of presents she couldn't live without. Everything seemed so normal until that Christmas Eve at her grandmother's house. The tiny village changed all that.

The snow village looked so peaceful and quiet, so unlike the Christmas she knew. Katherine wondered what made the village Christmas seem so different than hers, and deep inside she longed for it more than any toy in a Christmas catalog.

At nine o'clock, her mother called her away from the little village to go up-stairs and brush her teeth. Katherine did so without complaint, finally sliding into bed, which was really a few sheets and a blanket spread out on the floor next to her brothers and cousins.

Instead of laughing, giggling, and being warned by her parents to quiet down, she found herself staring at the dark ceiling, deaf to the laughter around her. All she could think about was the little, snow-covered village.

Two hours passed, then three. Katherine wondered if she'd ever fall asleep. It was quiet, and the only sound in the house was the faint sound of her grandpa's snoring.

B-o-n-g!

From somewhere, came the sound of a church bell. Katherine tried counting the deep clangs, but then a new sound caused her to stop as the bell continued to ring. She held her breath and listened.

It was laughter, children's laughter. Katherine sat up and peered into the darkness, but all she could see were the still forms of her cousins and brothers.

It must be someone in one of the other bedrooms, she thought. Without waking anyone around her, she tiptoed into the hallway and peeped into the other bedrooms.

That's weird, she thought. They're all asleep. Katherine started back to her room when she heard the unmistakable sound of laughter again.

It sounded like it was coming from just outside the front door so she hurried downstairs to investigate. Katherine was not especially brave, but something about the laughter sent her to the closet for her coat. Finding it, she slipped her arms in, zipped it up, and shoved a pink stocking cap down over her ears.

Without hesitation, she opened the door and stepped out onto the stoop. A few feet away, five giggling children tumbled in the snow. As she watched, she realized something was different...the neighborhood had changed.

They can't all be up, she thought. It's too late. But they were. The sidewalks were packed with people and the streets were busy with traffic. People were everywhere, shoveling their driveways, laughing, singing, and playing in the snow. There were even families skating on a nearby pond.

That's funny, she thought. I don't remember seeing a pond there before. I wonder how I could have missed it.

Bong! The bell rang again. As the sound echoed and faded, one of the children playing in the snow ran up to her. The boy's cheeks were cherry red from the cold.

"Do you want to play with us?" he asked. In the glow of the Christmas lights, Katherine could see his breath.

"Sure," she said and ran to join the others. She laughed when a snowball whizzed past her head, and returned fire, hitting the boy before he ducked behind a large, plastic Santa Claus.

Katherine and her new friends played, until suddenly one of them stopped and said, "It's time to go." Without explanation, the children ran off down the snowy sidewalk, laughing in the light of the towering streetlights.

Katherine thought she heard music in the air, but as she listened, all she could hear was the scraping sound of something large and heavy. She turned and saw an old, vaguely familiar truck plowing the snow-covered street.

"Hi, Katherine!" the driver called to her.

Katherine waved at the driver as the truck drove out of sight, leaving a perfectly carved path behind it.

It was then that Katherine realized that everyone in the street seemed to be walking in the same direction, like they were going to something. Curious by na-

ture, she followed them. As she walked, village people were decorating their homes with colorful lights, building snowmen, and getting ready for Christmas.

One little boy held the ladder for his father who was stringing lights from their front porch. The father smiled at Katherine as she walked by.

"Pretty night for a walk, Katherine," he said warmly. "Hope you find what you're looking for."

She smiled, confused by his comment.

I'm not looking for anything, she thought to herself, but then she wondered if maybe she really was.

She passed a cozy, white cottage and was startled to hear children running up behind her. Katherine turned and stepped off the sidewalk into the deep snow and watched as three children rushed by. Oddly enough, they were dressed as a Christmas tree, a star, and a Santa Claus. It was obvious they were in a hurry to get somewhere, and she watched silently as they shuffled down the sidewalk laughing.

"Come on, we're going to be late," she overheard the star say, and wasn't sure if he was talking to her or to the girl in the Christmas tree costume. Just to be sure she didn't miss anything, she walked faster.

The snowy sidewalk was packed with smiling people. It was like a parade:
children pulled sleds, a nanny with several children at her side pushed a baby buggy, and a string of ice skaters glided by holding onto each other's waists.

She was about to cross the street when a kind voice said, "Watch out, Katherine." Stopping quickly, she turned and saw that the voice belonged to a man driving a red tractor pulling a wagon filled with straw and children.

She smiled and thanked the driver.

How do all these people know my name, she wondered. Just then, she heard her name again. This time the voice came from a girl about Katherine's age, whose blonde hair hung in pigtails. The little girl walked behind her father, who was pulling a sled with a Christmas tree strapped on top.

She looked at Katherine and asked, "Are you going?"

"Going where?" Katherine answered.

"Come on," she said, "you'll find what you're looking for there."

"Why does everyone think I'm looking for something?" Katherine asked.

The girl and her father stopped, along with those who had been walking beside her. They stared at Katherine, and she felt uncomfortable by their looks.

In her best-friend-voice, the little girl urged, "Well, aren't you?"

As soon as the words were spoken, Katherine heard the deep clang of the church bell, and those around her resumed their journey, leaving Katherine standing in the falling snow. The crowd disappeared into the darkness.

"Come on, Katherine," a motherly voice called to her from somewhere far ahead.

Katherine was alone. At any other time she would have been scared to find herself in such a predicament, but standing on the snow-covered sidewalk, surrounded by thousands of Christmas lights, and the snow softly falling all around, she felt safe and brave.

She heard the beautiful music again, lovelier than any she had ever heard before. Closing her eyes to hear better, she felt a strong hand take hold of her shoulder. Startled, but not afraid, she whirled around and saw a tall man in a red jacket and brown hat.

"I'm sorry I startled you, Katherine," he said, as a gentle smile spread over his face, "but you looked like you could use some help."

"Can you take me to where the music is?" she asked.

"I'd be happy to," he answered. "Besides, it's a pretty night for a walk."

Unafraid, Katherine grabbed the man's hand. He smiled and listened as Katherine explained everything she had seen and heard. Almost in time to the music, the old bell clanged. It rang out loud and long, and just as the sound was about to die, it rang out again.

"Why does the bell ring so often?" she asked the man.

"You'll see," he said.

Katherine felt like saying, "Why doesn't anyone ever give me a real answer instead of saying, 'You'll see,' or 'you'll find out.'"

Before she knew it, Katherine and the man had come to the main part of town where the buildings stood close together and looked like they were out of a storybook.

A whistle blew as a policeman, with a red scarf wrapped around his neck, directed traffic. The officer waved his hand and winked a knowing wink as Katherine passed by.

Bong! The bell clanged again, and then it was quiet. The only sound she could hear was the crunch of soft snow beneath their feet.

"Just a little farther," the man said, pointing ahead. "Right up there past the train depot."

What Katherine saw looked more like a painting than real life. The depot was covered in tiny Christmas lights. Steam rose from the stack of a polished locomotive waiting at an empty platform, but there wasn't a soul in sight, which was odd since she had started the night wondering why so many people were out and about.

Bong! The bell rang again, even louder yet. Katherine wanted to cover her ears but was afraid to let go of the man's hand. Just as the sound died, they turned the corner and were greeted by a magnificent sight.

Everyone in the entire village stood clustered together with their backs to Katherine. This time, no one spoke. They stood quietly, facing a small white church with a tall bell tower on its peak.

Katherine longed to see what they were looking at. Standing on her tiptoes, Katherine hoped that by adding three inches to her height, she'd be able to see over the wall of grownups. Then, almost as though someone had signaled to the large group that Katherine was behind them, they all turned slowly to face her.

Without a word, the crowd parted and smiling faces lined the path leading to the church.

The man in the furry hat leaned down close to her face. "There's your answer," he whispered, pointing ahead.

Cautiously, Katherine started down the path of people that she had met that night. There was a smile on every face, but no one said anything.

Katherine made her way to the front of the church. Standing in the snow was a crudely made shack with a straw roof. In it, sat a man clothed in green and a woman dressed in blue.

Katherine walked to within a few feet of them, and the man and woman looked at her, and then shifted their gaze downward. Katherine eyes followed theirs until she found herself staring into the face of a little baby boy lying in a manger. She couldn't take her eyes off of him.

A hand touched her shoulder, and this time she knew it was the man in the brown hat. He knelt down, removed his hat, and with his eyes on the child said in a kind voice, "He is what you've been looking for."

Katherine knew he was right. She had known it as soon as she saw him lying there, his little legs wiggling in the tight wrappings. She knew it deep down in her heart, the place that no one can see except God. From overhead, the church bell tolled its familiar sound again.

"It's time to get you home," the man said.

As they walked, Katherine was blind to the beautifully still village because all she could picture was the little baby boy in the manger. She knew he was just a baby that belonged to one of the young mothers in the crowd, but she also knew who he was supposed to be.

Before she realized it, she was standing on the front step of her grandmother's house. Katherine guessed everyone was still asleep. Before going in, she turned to the man who had brought her home and wrapped her arms around his neck. She felt the soft fur of his hat on her cheek as she said, "I don't even know your name."

"Oh, that's not important," the man replied with a smile. "What is important is what you saw tonight. It's what you've been searching for, Katherine. Christmas isn't about lights, decorations, gifts, carols, or even snow. It's about HIM. It always has been, but folks have kind of forgotten that." He paused, and the smile left his face. "It's up to you, Katherine," he said, "to remind them."

With that, he stood straight and tall, picked up a large ax that was stuck in the snow, and quietly tromped away through the snow.

Katherine called out as loudly as she could without waking her family, "I won't forget!"

The man pulled up short and turned towards Katherine. "I know you won't," he said with a wink. He turned, walked off in the direction of the lodge near the pond, and disappeared.

Katherine went inside and returned to her spot amongst her brothers and cousins.

Once again, she found herself staring at the dark ceiling. As she thought about all that had happened, she couldn't get the baby in the manger out of her mind. All the twinkling lights, the beauty of the neighborhood, and the people she met in the snowy village were just foggy memories in comparison.

FISHERMAN'S NOOK
RESORT

Amidst her swirling thoughts and exhausted from her adventure, Katherine slipped into a delightful Christmas Eve sleep.

* * * * * * *

"Ouch!" she heard herself say. She opened her eyes and found her brother's bare foot in her face. It was Christmas morning, and the children hurried downstairs to open their gifts.

It took a few hours, but eventually the last present was opened. Kids and adults assembled toys and read directions. Grandpa sat in his chair, snacking on a few Christmas goodies that he was allowed to have since it was Christmas morning, and Grandma was busily cleaning up the mess that covered the entire house.

Katherine, tired from the previous night, found a nice, comfy place to rest near the Christmas tree and was startled to hear her grandmother call from the living room.

"Would you look at this?" she exclaimed, as everyone came running to see.

"Who did this?" she asked with a smile on her face. The tiny, village people had all been rearranged and were clustered in front of the white church where the child in a manger lay.

"Not me," said one of the twins.

"I didn't do it," added a cousin.

"Neither did we," they all said, accusing one another until everyone in the room had denied it.

"Well, then how did it happen?" she asked. A funny feeling crept over the room at the thought of the unexplainable mystery. One by one, they left the room in silence, trying to come to some reasonable explanation for this Christmas morning miracle.

Katherine was the last to leave. Wanting to get a closer look at the tiny village, she scooted a chair to the table and got as close as she could without bumping anything.

As she looked at the tiny, ceramic child lying in the manger, a lump rose in her throat, and tears welled up in her eyes.

Katherine was about to cry when something familiar caught her attention. Standing near the back of the tiny crowd, a solitary figure stood facing the child. The man wore a red jacket, a brown hat, and held an ax in one hand. Drawing her face close to him, she heard the familiar clang of an old church bell. She smiled and whispered to the little man, "I won't forget."

Katherine didn't forget. She still enjoys the smell of a freshly cut Christmas tree, making sugar cookies with little sprinkles, and singing Christmas carols, but now the center of her celebration is the Child who came to save the world.

The End

It's Called CHRISTMAS

Book Eight
of
The Familyman's Christmas Treasury

written by
TODD WILSON

illustrated by SAM WILSON

Loading Message

Hi. My name's Nook. I'm from the FUTURE. I've sent this secret message to you disguised as a story to keep the Powers from finding it. If they find out I've sent it back into the past, I could be erased.

I probably should start at the beginning…the future-beginning. Let me just say a lot has changed since your time. In the last three hundred years we've made a lot of progress. We now have colonies on Mars and live to be around 140. Most diseases have been wiped out, and we're extremely good looking…as you can tell from my picture. Unfortunately, we still don't have personal jet packs, they've outlawed pepperoni pizza, and…there's no such thing as Christmas. That's why I've sent this to you.

It all started about a year ago…

"Hey, out there in the past…how's the weather…do you really have to wash your own dishes…?"

"Stop it, Munch; I'm busy here…be quiet." Sorry. That was my kid brother, Munch. And yes, his name speaks for itself.

Like I was saying, it all started about a year ago, right around the holidays which happens to be my favorite time of year.

I love all the hype, the decorations, and of course, the gifts! My family has always made a huge deal about the Holiday and some of my best memories are opening presents around the tree.

About three weeks before the Holiday, I was at the Holiday Mall hoping to get one of those new Skydiscs for Munch.

I was lucky enough to snatch-up the last skydisc before an old lady in a hover chair could grab it. With my prize in hand, I zipped over to the Credits Exchanger to pay for it.

The guy behind the counter looked like he stepped out of a movie set from your time. His white hair was slicked back; he had old-fashioned glasses and wore a crisp, black bow tie. He smiled as he scanned the Skydisc.

"That'll be 1496 credits," he said nicely as I swiped my hand across the receiver. "Would you like it wrapped?"

"Nah, I'm in a hurry," I answered, thinking I'd do it later. "Happy Holiday."

Here's where the story really begins. Instead of handing me the disc, the old guy held onto it just long enough to slow me down. "It's called Christmas," he said deliberately.

"What?" I asked, having never heard that word in my whole life. But the guy just ignored my question, smiled, and said, "Have a great day."

I was out of there and stepped from the mall just as a People Mover pulled up to take me home. Normally, I'm not what you would call a deep-thinker, but there was just something about that guy's comment that rattled me.

"Maxine?" I said out loud since I was the only one in the Mover.

"Yes, Nook what can I do for you today?" the soothing voice said.

"Define Christmas."

removed," Maxine said.

Now, I've had Maxine search for about everything in the Milky Way and she has never once said something has been removed from the records.

"What do you mean removed?"

"Definition of removed – To take something away from the position previously occupied. To eliminate or get rid of."

"Yeah, I know what 'removed' means, but I mean…why would an entry be removed?

"Some entries have been removed from the uNet due to the hateful nature or offensiveness of the material."

"OK, I get that, but why was the word Christmas removed?" I was getting a little tired of the run around.

"I'm sorry but that answer is not found or has been removed."

"You've got to be kidding me!"

"Oh, would you like to hear a joke? How many robots does it take to screw in a plasma resist…?"

"No, I don't want to hear a joke; good bye, Maxine."

"Good bye, Nook, it has been a pleasure serving you."

That's whacked, I thought. The old guy didn't look like a rebel. He looked more like my grandfather. What could be so dangerous about the word Christmas that it had to be removed?

That's when I decided to do a little investigating. I started with my parents at dinner time. Lasagna had just hydrated, and we were sitting around the table when I decided this was as good a time as any to ask my question. "So does anyone know what Christmas is?"

It was like no one even heard me. Nothing. There was no shocked look on their faces like when I accidentally said the word…oh, never mind.

"What, Nook?" My Dad asked (yes, we still call them Mom and Dad). "What did you say? Chrysanthemums…?

"No, Christmas. I heard it today over at the Holiday Mall.

"Oooo, what were you getting at the mall?" Munch asked in his little, annoying brother voice.

"Nothing for you," I snapped, knowing he'd ask me at least a dozen more times before bed.

"I don't know," my dad answered, looking at my mom. "I've never heard the word Christmas before. Have you, Hun?"

"Don't ask me," she murmured, not the least bit intrigued by the unknown word. "Have you asked Maxine?"

"Yea, I asked, but she said it was gone."

"That's weird," my Dad said, "maybe the word is made up."

"Yeah, maybe," I said, "but the guy who said it to me didn't look like he was making it up."

The conversation ended, and I was right about one thing. Munch asked me at least twenty times if I had gotten him something at the mall. I said no each time…but threatened to take it back if he asked again.

Like I said, there was just something about that guy and his mysterious word that I couldn't shake.

At school the next day, I went straight to Ms. Goodright, my history teacher, and asked her about the word 'Christmas'. Again, there was nothing in her face that showed any sign of alarm like the time I…well, nevermind.

"Sorry, Nook, but I've never heard that word before."

Well, neither has Maxine. Do you think any old books would have some information?

"Let me check," she said. "We have several old dictionaries that might say something about it…" Her voice trailed off as she pulled up a screen and keyed in a search. "Hmm… that's odd."

"What's odd? Does it say anything?"

"No, nothing about Christmas, but it is mentioned in some of the older records…" her fingers raced over the screen as she searched deeper into the records. "Each text search leads to a…dead-end. Here's one mention of a document written almost five centuries ago about a famous work by Charles Dickens entitled A Christmas Carol, but when I search for the actual document, it's not there."

"What do you mean, not there?" I asked.

"Well, it certainly existed…it just doesn't exist anymore."

Ms. Goodright waded through the records for a good twenty minutes and then turned her attention fully to me. "Nook, I'd say that whatever Christmas was…it's been erased. My guess would be that it was removed because it was historically hateful or discriminating to other people groups. You see, many historical events have been permanently removed from the records because they are offensive to certain people groups or beliefs. It's one of the reasons all religions were eliminated several centuries ago.

"Do you think Christmas could have been erased at that time?"

"It's possible, but there is just no way of knowing."

"Doesn't that bother you?" I asked, sure that my history teacher would react with passion. "Why would something that's part of history be treated like it wasn't?"

"That's the beauty of historical interpretation," she said calmly. "Sometimes you emphasize certain aspects and minimize other ones in order to include all people. I mean how would it benefit others to talk about some of the hatred and discrimination of the past? One of the reasons why war has been eliminated is because, unlike the civilizations of that past, we have learned to not only tolerate other views but also to silence those voices that create strife and discord."

This was starting to sound like an impromptu history class and I kind of got lost in the argument. The only thing that wasn't lost was my interest in finding out what Christmas really meant.

It was time to go back to the source.

As soon as school let out, I was back on a Mover to the Holiday Mall and on a mission to find the old clerk and ask what he knew about Christmas.

"Where is that guy?" I wondered, scanning the store. I hung around for a good two hours with no luck; the old guy wasn't at the check-out belt. I was on my way out when I bumped into the very person I had come to find.

"Hey, you're the person I'm looking for," I exclaimed, a little surprised to be standing face to face with the clerk.

It was obvious from his expression that he didn't have a clue who I was. "Can I help you young man?"

"Yeah, I was here yesterday and bought a skydisc for my brother…"

"Oh, returns can be made through the uNet or you can take the item…"

"I don't want to return it."

"Then what seems to be the trouble?" he asked pleasantly.

"Yesterday, when I paid for the skydisc, I said, "Happy Holiday"…and you said, "It was called Christmas." As the words left my lips, the man's mood changed and he leaned into my face.

"No, that's what it IS called, but we can't talk about it right here." The smile returned to his face and he glanced around to see if anyone might be listening. "If you'd like to learn more, you can meet me at "Tony's" this evening at 7 o'clock." Tony's served the best artichoke and soybean pizza on the planet. "My treat," he added.

7:10 - Tony's

After three slices of pizza I finally asked, "So what's Christmas?"

The old guy across the table removed his glasses and set them on the table. He leaned in trying to direct the conversation to my ears only. "It's NOT so much about 'what it is' but 'WHO it's about', he said. He looked around him and then reached into the inside pocket of his jacket and…PULLED OUT A BLASTER!!

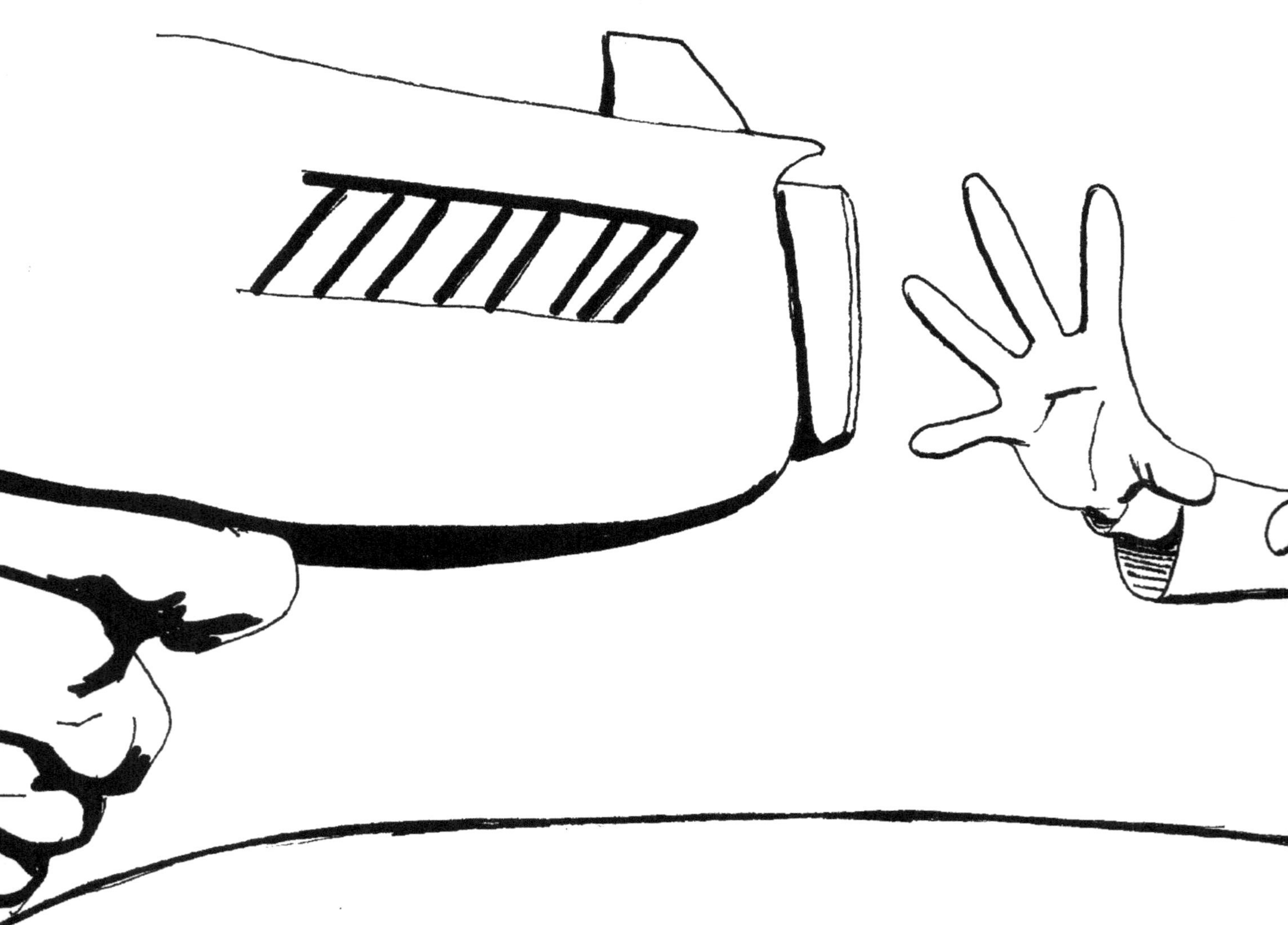

No, I'm just kidding! We don't even have blasters…which would be so cool if we did. Anyway, he reached into his pocket and pulled out something wrapped in a cloth (he later told me the cloth was something called a handkerchief).

Carefully, he unwrapped the object. I looked at it…and had no idea what it was.

"So what's that?" I asked pointing to the…thing, on the table.

"It's made from ceramic and is over 300 years old."

"Yeah, I can tell it's old, but what IS it?"

"Actually, it's only one piece from an entire set. It was passed down to me from my grandfather who received it from his grandfather who got it from his…"

"Yeah, but what is it?!" Old people are so slow.

"It's a ceramic figurine of a baby lying in a manger. Mangers were used as feeding troughs for animals."

"So why is a baby laying in an animal food tray?"

"Manger."

"Sure. So why is the baby laying in a manger?"

"That my young friend…is Christmas." He smiled and eased back into his seat.

"That's Christmas?!" I said a little disappointed and confused. The old guy leaned forward and continued, "Yes, that's Christmas.

This child is the reason the word Christmas has been removed from all the records. You have checked, haven't you?"

"Yep…nothing."

"Nothing," he echoed. "You see the Powers don't want to acknowledge this baby, His birth, or what He offers."

Ok, so now I'm getting interested. "Who's the kid?"

The smile left the man's face as though I had said something offensive, like when I said… oh, nevermind. "This child is not just any child…He is God's Son. His name is Jesus. He came to save us. Nook, he came to save YOU."

"What do you mean he came to save me? Save me from what?" This was starting to feel a little creepy.

"Something you were born with, Nook. Something we were all born with…sin."

"What do you mean, sin?"

"Sin is all the bad stuff that we do, that we think, and that we were born with. It separates us from God. Oh, that name may be old fashioned and laughed at, but you know what I say is true, Nook. They may have eliminated God from all the records, but you know that He exists…don't you?"

I felt my head nod in agreement. I knew God was an idea from the past and that no one ever mentioned Him anymore…but sometimes, when I lay in bed in the dark…I knew there had to be something bigger. I just knew God had to be there…somewhere.

"You see, they can erase it from everything, but they cannot erase the truth." He paused and looked to one side. "But it gets better. Not only does God exist, but He even revealed Himself through a book called the Bible."

I had heard about the Bible, but it was always talked about like it was some voodoo book from the past. And, I had never even seen one…until now. The old guy reached in his pocket and removed a small, tattered book and set it beside the ceramic figurine.

It lay in the open for just a few seconds when suddenly the old guy scooped up the Bible and the figurine and shoved them back in his pockets. "I'm afraid we'll have to continue this conversation at a later date."

"What? We just started this conversation…what's so bad about this Jesus and why would they want to erase him from the records…AND WHAT DOES ALL THIS HAVE TO DO WITH CHRISTMAS!!" I must have been getting loud because people looked over at our table.

The old guy laughed and put his finger to his lips to quiet me. Then he whispered, "You are in danger when you speak so loudly." The guy pulled out a scrap of paper and began writing.

"Man, I haven't seen anyone write on paper in forever," I said, amazed that he still knew how.

"This is safer," he said and handed me the note. "We're having a little…Holiday Party on Sunday at this address, and you're invited. I think you'll find it…interesting." He stood and gathered his coat. "It was a pleasure talking with you, Nook. I hope your brother enjoys his Skydisc." He took my hand in his and leaned down casually and whispered, "Merry Christmas."

"OK, this is getting weirder by the minute," I mumbled to myself. I was talking to a crazy, old guy about God and His Son, and he said it was dangerous. I like dangerous…but I don't like DANGEROUS.

Over the next four days I went back and forth as to what to do. When the time came, I told my parents I was going to a Holiday party and would be back later. Getting out of the Mover and walking to the front door, I had the sinking feeling that this might turn out bad.

When the door to the house opened I was greeted by a pretty, dark-haired girl who was about my age. "Hi, you must be Nook," she said. "Mr. Z told us you would be coming." I stepped in and wondered if the old guy was Mr. Z. "Sounds like a secret code name," I thought.

The girl led me to large, open room filled with about twenty people sitting around the edges of the room. "Nice holiday tree," I said pointing to the large decorated tree in the corner of the room.

"Thanks," she said with a smile, "but it's a Christmas tree."

"Nook!" a familiar voice called out. "I'm so glad that you were able to make it." It was the old guy sitting near the Holiday tree with the old book on his knee. "I see you've met Ally… these are her parents Robert and Mia," he said, pointing to the nice looking couple next to him. Then he made his way around the room and introduced the others.

I sat down beside a short, dark man named Paul and was surprised to learn that he worked in the office with my dad.

"Well, I'm glad everyone could make it," Mr. Z began. "I thought we'd begin with a song. I know most of you know this one, but this is going to be new for Nook."

I pulled up the screen on my wristband for the lyrics but was stopped by Mr. Z. "You might as well put that away Nook; we use paper…it's safer."

I was handed a small square of paper with words written on it. Mr. Z was right; this song was new to me.

"Away in the Manger," Ally said and then looked at me, "Maxine doesn't know this one, Nook, so don't ask her." She smiled, and I smiled back having no clue what she was talking about.

Soft music filled the room and then everyone sang.

They sang on telling the story of Christmas. What struck me most wasn't so much the words but the way everyone sang. Mr. Z's eyes were closed and Paul was crying.

"What is going on?" I wondered.

After the last words were sung, Mr. Z opened his old book and looked right at me. "Nook, in this book God tells us how He sent His son, Jesus, to save the world. He came as a baby and for over thirty years He lived among the people revealing God through himself…and then He died a terrible death on a cross for our sins. He died for you, Paul, Ally, her parents, all of us, and for the whole world. But the world hated Him as much then as they do now and have erased Him and His story. Nook, Christmas is the celebration of His birth…of Him. Over decades and centuries, little by little, things were altered and truths twisted until all that was left was an empty holiday, filled with meaningless traditions. But even if the reason, the story, and the name are forgotten…it is still called Christmas, because it's all about Christ."

To tell you the truth, I still didn't understand what they were talking about. We sang a few more songs about Jesus' birth and read out of 'the' book. I left the party and that would have been the end of it if what happened a few weeks later hadn't happened, but something did happen...and that changed everything.

Two days before the Holiday I got this message: "Nook, Ally is calling."

"Thanks, Maxine, I'll take the call."

"Nook here," I answered.

"Hi Nook, this is Ally...from the party two weeks ago..." she sounded anxious.

"Yeah, how's it going?" I said trying to sound charming.

"Can I meet you somewhere this afternoon?"

"I can stop by your house..."

"No, that's not good," she interrupted. "How about the park at three?"

"Sure, that'll work. See you th.."

"Call ended unexpectedly," Maxine said. "Would you like to call back?"

"No."

Stepping from the Mover, I saw Ally sitting on a park bench near a clump of trees. With all the charisma I could muster, I plopped down beside her and said, "Hey Ally, what's up?"

She jumped in surprise and looked around her before speaking. "Mr. Z is gone," she announced abruptly.

"He died?" I asked, shocked by her words.

"No. Just gone." she said looking right into my eyes. "He didn't show up for our last Holiday meeting…and I checked at the Holiday Mall, and they said there was no one who worked there by that name. I even called his home and the number has been discontinued."

"Where do you think he went?"

"I don't know, but I'm scared…and my parents are scared, too. They said they were afraid something like this would happen…and now it has."

"What do you mean they thought something like this would happen? What are you talking about?"

"Don't you see it yet, Nook. The Powers don't want Christmas, God, or Jesus. They've erased Him from everything, and they will erase anyone who causes trouble."

"Come on! You think Mr. Z was taken out because of Christmas?"

"Think about it. You can't find it on the records, the uNet…anywhere. And then Mr. Z starts saying to people at the store, "It's called Christmas." You weren't the first person you know. All of us: my parents, Paul, the Neal's, Cal, Jed, and the rest…they all came because of Mr. Z and now he's gone."

Suddenly, I felt afraid too. "Have you heard from the rest?"

"Just my parents…no one else." She paused and then held out a small box wrapped in holiday wrapping. "Nook, this was delivered to the house yesterday…and it has your name on it."

Reluctantly, I took the package from her trembling hands. "What do you think it is?" I asked.

"I don't know, but we think it's from Mr. Z."

"How do you know?"

"See that X under your name?" she said pointing to the label on the

package. "A really long time ago the X was a sign for Christ. They even called Christmas, X-mas."

Now, I felt afraid-er and looked around to see if anyone might be looking…and it seemed to me that EVRYONE was looking at us. In a wave of fear, I leaned forward and wrapped my arms around Ally and said for others to hear, "Thanks for the Holiday gift…are you sure I can't open it now? " Ally looked a little bewildered but played along.

"Yeah, you have to wait until the Holiday."

I got up and wondered if she enjoyed the hug as much as I did. From the look on her face, I was guessing…no.

"See you later?" I asked.

"Yeah, we're supposed to have a Holiday party the day after the Holiday at Paul's apartment. That is…if he's still there."

"Send me the address," I said and left.

"I will," she said. "Nook, be careful."

"You too," I said, trying to smile.

That night I went to my room and opened the package. It was Mr. Z's old book. A note was tucked within the pages. A tremble ran through my body as I unfolded the crisp paper.

"Nook, I've sent you this because I think my time is limited. Don't be afraid; every

word in this book is true, and I know God has a plan for you. I've marked a place in the book for you to start reading. Read all the way to the end. It's up to you to remind them, Nook. Be careful, watch out for each other, and remind them... it's called Christmas."

Merry Christmas, Mr. Z

I sat there on the edge of my bed stunned by the realization. They took him away. He was…erased.

I opened the old book where it was marked and read the ancient and faded words. "While they were there, the time came for the baby to be born, and she gave birth to her firstborn, a son. She wrapped him in cloths and placed him in a manger, because there was no guest room available for them."

Well, to make a long story short, it took me a couple of months to finish 'the' book. But I did. With the help of the others, who were all still safe, I learned why Jesus came, how He died for me, and that all He wants me to do is …believe…and tell others about Him…and about Christmas.

That's what I've been doing ever since…

"ME TOO!!!! Me TOO!!! Merry Christmas everyone in the past!!!"

"Not so loud, Munch…" Yes, the rest of my family, including Munch, believes too. I had to tell them…they're my family. That's when I started thinking, if I could send a message to you in the PAST, maybe you could stop it from happening in the FUTURE. Here's a freaky thought for you: maybe YOU can keep Christmas from being erased.

As I've learned from others, they've already begun to erase it in your time. Look around and you'll see it happening. Of course they won't go about it in a loud way, but in lots of smaller, softer ways. They'll erase a little at a time until Jesus, God, and Christmas have been ignored and forgotten altogether.

Whatever you do, don't let that happen.

The next time you're at a mall and a check-out person says, "Happy Holiday," remind them of what an old guy once said to me, "It's called Christmas."

I gotta go. Hope this works. Nook, signing out!! Man I always wanted to say that.

"Merry Christmasssssssss!!!!"

That was Munch, again.

The Christmas Bowl

Book Nine
of
The Familyman's Christmas Treasury

written by
TODD WILSON

illustrated by SAM WILSON

Cal and Jed were about as close as two brothers could be. They played together, talked together, wrestled together, and sometimes fought together. Cal stuck up for Jed when needed, and Jed looked up to his big brother. They lived in an old, brick house on the edge of town. The brothers thought it was the best place to live in the whole world. And it was.

Across the street from their house was a railroad track. Sometimes the boys walked the tracks with their dad to pick up old metal treasures, balance on the iron rails, or leave pennies on the track, hoping to find flattened pieces of copper in their place. On the other side of the tracks, just south of town, lived an old man named Marshall Griswold.

He lived by himself in a brick house that looked like the big bad wolf could easily blow down. Huge trees had grown up around it and the grass looked like it hadn't been cut in years. Cal and Jed's dad said Mr. Griswold fell off a mower a long time ago and cut his

leg real bad, which is why he walked with a limp. The boys guessed that he was afraid to cut the grass after that. Behind the house was an old, dilapidated barn that looked like it might collapse at any moment.

About the only time the boys ever saw the old man was at the post office or on Sundays as he drove by on his way to church. A red, dented mailbox stood at the end of his driveway. Underneath it, hanging from a rusty wire, was a painted, wooden sign that read "wooden bowls for sale". The weather had worn away some of the letters but apparently people could still read it because Cal and Jed saw cars pull across the railroad tracks and up to his house. Their dad said that Mr. Griswold was probably the best wooden bowl maker around.

One chilly, Saturday morning in early December, their dad secretly announced, "Boys, we're going to do something special today." He told them that he planned to buy a bowl from Mr. Griswold as a Christmas gift for their mom…and it was to be a secret.

They would go see Mr. Griswold while their mom ran errands that morning. So when they heard the door shut, the three of them ran to the window to see her get into the car and pull away. As soon as her car was out of sight, their Dad barked in his fake, military voice, "All right troops; begin operation Christmas bowl. We leave at 0900." He tried to look serious although he had no idea what 0900 meant.

Cal and Jed went upstairs to their bedrooms, got dressed, and brushed their teeth. They forgot to comb their hair, but it was short and their dad didn't care. Their dad put on his overalls, which he liked to wear on Saturdays, and they all went pounding down the creaky stairs, out the door, and into the car.

They turned at the mailbox, crossed the railroad tracks, and stopped next to Mr. Griswold's house. Cal and Jed were nervous about meeting Mr. Griswold. The car stopped and their dad said, "Come on boys, let's go!" Cal and Jed scrambled out of the car and made their way to the front door. Their dad knocked, reminding them to be polite and not touch anything. No one came to the door so their dad knocked again, this time more loudly. "Well, let's try out by the barn; he's got to be here… there's his truck," he said. They made their way to the barn and they heard a shuffle coming from behind the door. The door opened and their stood Mr. Griswold filling the doorway. Mr. Griswold smiled a big smile as though he was expecting them. "Hi, Mr. Griswold," their dad said. "We live across the tracks right down the way in that brick house with the white stripe around it.

These are my sons Caleb and Jedidiah."

Mr. Griswold looked down at Cal and Jed and said, "Hi Caleb and Jedidiah; I'm Marshall Griswold. What can I do for you this fine day?"

"We were wondering if we could buy a wooden bowl for my wife as a Christmas present," their dad answered.

"Come on in," Mr. Griswold said, without answering his question.

It was dark as they stepped out of the sunshine, but a moment later their eyes adjusted to the warmly lit barn. It was small, had a few windows on one side, and a cluttered work bench on the other. Near the center of the room stood a rusty, wood-burning stove that filled the barn with a good-smelling heat. On shelves near the work bench, there were a dozen beautiful, wooden bowls unlike anything the boys had ever seen.

There was a golden brown bowl, some dark bowls, some almost black or red, and one was even white. The odd thing about them was that each one had tiny dark holes scattered all over them. It looked like someone had cut little designs with the tiniest saw in the world. Cal and Jed wondered how Mr. Griswold made the designs without shattering the bowls and hoped they could see him make one.

"Well," their Dad said a little awkwardly, "can I choose any of these bowls to buy for my wife?"

Mr. Griswold smiled and gestured to the beautiful bowls, "One of these bowls? No, I'm afraid not; these bowls are all spoken for," he said as he walked over to the shelf of bowls.

"This one is for a lady out west who stopped in here last summer," he said holding one of the dark bowls in his worn hands. "And this one belongs to the Widow Johnson down the street," he said as he picked up the white bowl. "I'm giving it to her for her 95th birthday. And this one…," he said, as he cradled a dark red bowl in his hands that looked old and as smooth as silk, "I made for my wife as a gift. It took me several weeks to carve, but she passed away a week before I finished it." Mr. Griswold got kind of quiet as he looked at that bowl.

"I'm sorry about your wife," the boys' dad said.

"She had been sick for a while…but now she is in heaven, and I'm glad," Mr. Griswold said and then added, "But I sure do miss her."

Their Dad spoke next, "Ummm… are there ANY bowls that don't belong to someone already?"

Without even looking at the shelf of bowls Mr. Griswold answered, "No, they all have a home, but I'd be happy to make one for you. So you said you need it in time for Christmas?"

"That'll be fine," he said. "I'll have it done for you by then—one thing though, I'll need your boys to help me, if that's OK with you," he asked with a playful gleam in his eyes.

"Well sure, that'd be great!" their Dad answered without even asking them.

"They'd love to help; when will you start?"

Mr. Griswold lifted his hand to his chin and screwed up his face trying to figure the whole thing out. "We'll start Monday afternoon, right after school. Is that OK with you boys?"

"Sure," they answered, without even checking with their dad.

"They'll be here!" their dad added. Mr. Griswold shook hands with their dad, then Cal, and then bent down to Jed and tousled his head of blond hair.

As they pulled back in their driveway, their dad said, "Mom will never know we were gone. It looks like this is going to work out perfectly. Now remember, we can't let Mom know what we're doing."

"We know," they said.

Over the weekend the boys whispered to each other about going to Mr. Griswol Jed almost let it slip when his mom was cleaning out the wooden bowl that sat on fireplace. He started to say something, but Cal grabbed his arm and looked at h sternly.

On Monday after school, the boys asked their Mom if they could walk do the railroad tracks and look for train stuff. They had done that dozens of times, s didn't seem like a strange thing to ask, and their unsuspecting Mother told then be careful and to stay away from the creek.

Cal and Jed nodded in agreement and took off out the door, ran across the street, and started down the tracks in the direction of Mr. Griswold's. All at once an unexpected fear caught up with them and they had second thoughts about going with old Mr. Griswold. For all they knew this might be a trap to change them into monsters or something.

"Come on Jed," Cal said. They made their way to the old barn door where they had first met Mr. Griswold. Cal lifted his hand to knock but before his hand hit the door, it swung open, and out stepped Mr. Griswold.

"Hi boys," he said with a big smile. The wrinkles on his face crinkled up and the mustache that hung over his lip turned upward making his smile look even bigger. "Are you ready to go get your Mom's Christmas bowl?" he asked. He slapped a big, red, flannel cap on his head and picked up a carved walking stick leaning against the wall. Cal and Jed nodded in unison. "Oh," he said, "we'll need one more thing." He stepped back into the doorway and emerged holding two smaller, carved, walking sticks. He handed one to Cal that had a carved bear's head on top and one to Jed with a lion's head.

"You'll need these where we're going."

His comment troubled the boys. They assumed they were going to stay at the barn and watch as he made the bowl, but now he was taking them somewhere.

They followed
Mr. Griswold as he
walked past the old,
red truck and in the
direction of the woods
behind the barn. They passed
old farm machinery, an old bath tub,
a rusty bicycle, and a huge stack of freshly-cut
firewood. "Before we can make the bowl, we have to
find just the right piece of wood," Mr. Griswold said. He took
long strides as he walked towards the woods and Cal and Jed half
ran to keep up. Just before they entered the woods, Mr. Griswold
stopped and said, "Well boys, we'd better stop and ask God to show
us the perfect piece of wood for your mother's Christmas bowl." He
removed his hat and bowed his head as he leaned heavily on
the carved walking stick. Cal and Jed did the same.

"Father, would you please guide us to
the perfect piece of wood for this special
Christmas bowl? In Your Son's name, I
pray. Amen." Cal and Jed raised their
heads. Mr. Griswold replaced his hat
and said with a wink, "Let's go find

that piece of wood". They took off into the woods ahead of Mr. Griswold, although neither of them had any idea what they were looking for. After a few minutes of searching, Jed came over to Mr. Griswold and asked, "What exactly are we looking for?"

Mr. Griswold looked up smiling and said, "I'll just know".

Cal yelled out from 20 yards away, "I found a big piece!" Jed and Mr. Griswold made their way to Cal. He was standing on a big log that must have been three feet around. It was dark brown inside and Cal asked, "How 'bout this one?" Mr. Griswold studied it for a moment and said that it was a fine specimen of walnut but it wasn't quite right.

"We'd better keep looking," he said. So they did.

A while later, Jed and Cal saw Mr. Griswold sizing up a tall tree with branches spread wide. They made their way over to him as he looked up into the tree.

"What kind of tree is it?' Jed asked.

"Chestnut," Mr. Griswold answered. "It makes good bowls, but I don't think this is the wood for your Mother's Christmas bowl." Cal and Jed looked at each other and wondered how much longer this would take. The three of them spent about two hours in the woods when Mr. Griswold finally said, "Well, we'd better get you boys home."

Cal asked, "But what about the wood for my Mom's bowl?"

"It looks like you'll have to come back tomorrow, and we'll look some more," he said as though it didn't bother him one bit that they had spent two hours looking for a piece of wood. "Can you boys come back after school tomorrow?"

"I guess," Cal said. "We'll have to ask our Dad."

"Fine," Mr. Griswold said as he collected their walking sticks. "I'll see you boys tomorrow."

The boys' Mom greeted them in the kitchen. "Did you find anything?" she asked. The boys thought she knew they were looking for wood and Cal was about to say, "How did you know?" when he realized she was talking about train stuff.

"No," Cal said we didn't find a thing. Cal wanted to make sure he wasn't lying. After all, it was true that they hadn't found a single thing. After dinner, the boys told their dad what had happened and that they were going to have to go back tomorrow.

Their dad was a little surprised but said, "Then I guess you'll go back tomorrow."

After school, Cal asked his Mom if they could go walk the railroad tracks again. This would have caused suspicion on any other day because she would be surprised that they wanted to do the same thing two days in a row— they were like that. But at this moment she was trying to change a very

messy diaper. She had hardly said "yes" when they shot out the door.

Mr. Griswold must have seen them coming because before they got to the door, he had swung it open and smiled that big smile of his. "God has given us a great day to look for your mother's Christmas bowl." There wasn't a cloud in the sky and a crisp, late, autumn wind blew a refreshing smell from somewhere.

After handing them their sticks, Mr. Griswold started off toward the woods. They passed the junk and wood piles which had been added to since they walked by yesterday. They got to the edge of the wood and were about to take off running when Mr. Griswold came to a stop and removed his hat and said, "Let's ask God to guide us to the perfect piece of wood."

"Father, we ask you to point us to the perfect piece of wood for this very special Christmas bowl, in Your Son's name we pray, Amen." His prayers were always short and simple, but both boys felt as though God must have been very close as he prayed. With a nod of his head, the boys took off in one direction and Mr. Griswold walked in another. For the next hour, the three of them walked and hollered, laughed and talked about wood, bowls, and other things. But as the sun was going down they still hadn't found the right piece of wood. They had seen plenty of wood but nothing that Mr. Griswold thought was worthy of their special Christmas bowl.

Mr. Griswold called them in and they made the trip back to the barn where he collected their walking sticks, told them to be back the next day if they could, and then stepped inside the barn door and left them standing outside. They turned and made their way home, and all that night they were quietly wondering if they were ever going to find the right piece of wood.

The next day they did just as they had the previous two days and made their way down to Mr. Griswold's. Mr. Griswold opened the door before they arrived at the door, flashed a big smile, and said, "This is going to be the day boys, I just know it." He handed them their walking sticks and with his in hand, began the walk toward the woods, but this time he angled off just a bit to the right towards a spot that looked a older and thicker than the rest of the woods.

They came to the edge of the woods, and the boys stopped even before Mr. Griswold did, knowing what he was about to do. He lifted his hat, bowed his head, and prayed, "Father, we've been looking for two days now and we would sure like to get on with making this bowl. Guide us to the perfect piece of wood for this special bowl, in Your Son's name we pray, Amen." Let's go, he said.

After about an hour, Cal walked over to where Jed sat against a tree. "What's wrong?" Cal asked.

"I'm tired of looking for this perfect piece of wood," he said. "Why can't we just pick a piece and make the bowl—what does it matter?"

Just as he said that, Mr. Griswold came over to where the boys were, and just as Jed was about to tell Mr. Griswold the same thing he had just told Cal, Mr. Griswold smiled his big smile and said with a gleam in his eye, "It looks like God has led you to the perfect piece of wood."

"Where?" the boys asked at the same time, looking around as if expecting to see a sign with a big red X on it.

"Jed's sitting on it," he said as he tapped the chunk of wood under Jed with his walking stick. The boys looked down, and Jed jumped up quickly as though he was sitting on a hot stove.

"That's it?" Cal said. "That's about the ugliest piece of wood that I've ever seen." In fact, it was the ugliest piece of wood he had ever seen. It was about the size of their dad's tool box and looked like a bulge on the side of a bicycle tire.

Mr. Griswold smiled knowing something they didn't. "It's called a burl." he said. "It's like a big knot that has been growing on that old tree for a long time. That's what we'll make your mom's Christmas bowl out of." The boys couldn't believe that anything pretty could ever come out of that ugly chunk of wood. "I'll come back tomorrow morning and get this burl and tomorrow after school, we'll start making your mom's bowl."

"First we need to thank God for leading us here." As the sun shone through the bare branches, the three of them prayed thanking God for this ugly but special piece of wood. After Mr. Griswold said Amen, the three of them walked, skipped, and ran all the way back to the barn. Mr. Griswold collected their walking sticks. "I've had a good day with you boys," he said. "See you tomorrow."

The next day, the sky was gray and heavy as the boys came towards the door of the barn. The door swung open and Mr. Griswold smiled a big smile and said, "Well boys, are you ready to start working on your mom's Christmas bowl?"

"Yeah," they answered. He ushered them inside and closed the door behind them.

As their eyes adjusted to the light, they spotted the bowls that sat gracefully on the old, dusty shelves. Cal noticed that the white bowl was gone. The boys stood still waiting for their instructions, and Jed fought the urge to kick a large pile of wood chips near his feet.

Mr. Griswold showed them to the old work bench that sat in the middle of the room. "This bench used to be my dad's. He taught me how to make wooden bowls, and he was the best."

"I did a little work on it this morning," he said. He turned to a square block of wood that sat on the dark workbench. "I cut off the bark and now it's at the point where we can begin to shape it into a bowl." The block of wood was light colored with dark swirls through it and tiny dark spots all over it. They still couldn't believe that they had searched for three days to find this piece of wood. Mr. Griswold smiled and gently rubbed his hand across the block.

Before we begin, he said, "I have a job for you two." The boys assumed it was some kind of important job but when He added, "There is a broom and a dust pan over in the corner," they realized it wasn't going to be important at all. "The shop needs to be swept clean before we begin," he said. As they swept, Mr. Griswold brushed off the work bench sweeping more wood chips and saw dust onto the floor.

They spent about thirty minutes cleaning the place and after the last dust pan of sawdust was thrown away and the broom was put away, Mr. Griswold gave the shop a quick look and said, "Good job boys, it hasn't looked this clean in years." He let loose another of his big smiles as he rumpled up Jed's hair.

Mr. Griswold carried the block of wood to a big old piece of machinery. "This is a lathe.'" Mr. Griswold said. "It spins the wood real fast and then we use different chisels to carve out the inside as well as the outside of the bowl." The boys perked up at the thought of a spinning block of wood and the possibility of using really sharp chisels. "I spent the better part of the morning sharpening these chisels," he said as he picked up a large chisel.

He held it up to his eye and then lightly brushed his thumb against the blade. "Yep, you've gotta have sharp tools to make good bowls." The boys were beginning to get the idea that it takes a lot of time just to get to the point where you get to start working on a bowl.

Mr. Griswold gently lifted the big block of wood and placed it into the jaws of the old machine. He turned some knobs, made some adjustments, and spun the block of wood in the machine by hand, examining it as it spun.

"Keep your hands away from the lathe," he said and as he let Jed push the button that made the machine jump to life. It made a soft whirring sound, and Mr. Griswold brought his face down level with the block and stared at it as it spun. After a minute, he stood up straight and winked at the two brothers and said, "I think we're ready to start."

"Let's pray," he said quietly. "Father, you've lead us to the perfect piece of wood and for that we thank you again. Now we ask you to make our hands work skillfully and that you would be pleased by our work...." Mr. Griswold paused as though he were ready to say, "Amen" but then added something else he wanted to say "...and Lord, thank you for bringing along Cal and Jed. It's been real nice being with them. In Jesus' name I pray, Amen." He opened his eyes and said, "Well, boys, here we go."

The boys smiled at Mr. Griswold as he picked up the chisel that looked like a sharp spoon and set it on a metal work rest near the spinning wood. A shower of shavings pealed from the wooden block as a scraping sound filled the old barn. The old man's hands moved gracefully and looked strong as he tipped the chisel from time to time to get it to cut like he wanted. It was beginning to look more bowl-like already.

He worked while they watched. Occasionally, Jed would bend over and pick up a handful of sawdust and throw it at Cal until Cal

would say, "Stop it, Jed." Mr. Griswold worked for about an hour. The block of wood had become a bowl, although the inside was still filled with wood. It was light in color and a fine dust covered it which made it look dull. Cal touched it lightly and felt its smoothness. "That's enough for now," Mr. Griswold said. "We'll finish it tomorrow. Let's clean up these wood shavings and then how 'bout I get us some cookies that I have in the house?"

Cal grabbed the broom in the corner and Jed picked up the dust pan while Mr. Griswold disappeared from the barn to get their snack. In no time at all, the wood chips were deposited in a trash can and Mr. Griswold returned carrying some cookies in a red cardboard box. In his other hand, he held a pitcher and a couple of glasses. They sat down and Mr. Griswold poured the glasses full of milk and opened the box of cookies. And then they did something that they had never done before with Mr. Griswold. They ate cookies, drank milk, and talked. He asked them about school and their hobbies and they asked him about his father and his wife.

They laughed and talked for about an hour when Mr. Griswold looked at the big watch on his wrist and announced, "Boys you'd better get going. Your Mom's probably wondering where you are. We don't want her thinking something's fishy," he said. "We'll finish tomorrow." Jed handed his empty glass to Mr. Griswold while Cal took one more long drink.

Jed said cheerfully, "I sure had fun today."

"Me too," Mr. Griswold said thoughtfully, as if he hadn't had that much fun in a long time. "See you tomorrow."

The next day, just as before, the door swung open. Mr. Griswold smiled a big smile and said, "Hello Boys!" and then whisked them into the barn.

Mr. Griswold turned to the boys and stooped down putting one hand on his knee and the other on Cal's shoulder. With a big smile he said, "Were just about finished."

Still attached to the lathe, the bowl looked soft. The sides sloped gently out. Cal reached out and touched it. It was powdery smooth. Mr. Griswold smiled almost forgetting that he had created it. "There are only two things left to do," he said. He picked up a saw and cut at the base of the bowl until it was

freed from the grasp of the lathe. Mr. Griswold held it in his hand like an archeologist might hold a treasure unearthed from a Pharaoh's tomb. Both boys noticed those same tiny holes in the bowl that the finished bowls on the dusty shelves had. Mr. Griswold said, "One more thing to do."

He walked over to another part of the shop that held old, dark, paint cans. The labels were unreadable but Mr. Griswold picked one out without hesitation. With the bowl in one hand and the can in the other, he came back to the old workbench and set them down. He picked up an old, worn down screw driver and pried off the lid and it smelled of old paint. Mr. Griswold asked Cal to pick up a long narrow scrap of wood that lay on the shop floor and hand it to him. Cal of course did as he was told and Mr. Griswold dipped the stick into the can and began slowly stirring the can as he looked in it. As he stirred, he began softly humming to himself. Cal recognized the tune of a Christmas carol that they sang in church, although he couldn't remember the words.

When Mr. Griswold was satisfied, he stopped and scraped some of the excess brown liquid from the stick and set it on the workbench. He walked over to a rusty filing cabinet and pulled a clean rag from it and skipped back over to the bench in excitement.

"You're getting better at skipping," Jed said.

"Thanks, I've been practicing," he said as they laughed. Taking the clean rag, Mr. Griswold folded it a certain way and then gingerly dipped it into the mouth of the can and pulled it back out and waited as a few drops of brown liquid fell into the can. With his empty hand, he picked up the almost finished bowl and touched the rag to the bowl. Something magical happened, for as he wiped the rag against the light colored bowl, a trail of glistening dark wood was left in its path. He continued to wipe on the stain, filling in all the spots he missed and to the boys' astonishment, the bowl began to change right before their eyes.

As he buffed and stained, and stained and buffed, the bowl began to glow in the light of the barn. Mr. Griswold gingerly laid the bowl down trying not to mar the lustrous finish. As he did, the boys' eyes followed the bowl to the table. They stood staring at it, not knowing that Mr. Griswold had quit looking at his creation and now looked at the two brothers who had become so special to him. They couldn't believe their eyes. The bowl was curved up slightly at the edges and tiny dark holes were scattered all over its surface. It reminded Cal of a mushroom that grew on the side of a tree in their back yard. Jed thought it looked like fairies had carved it and left it on Mr. Griswold's back stoop for him to find. To both of them, it looked like magic had been used to make it.

Mr. Griswold spoke softly, "It turned out real pretty, didn't it, boys?" The boys' eyes were still fixed on the wooden bowl and neither one answered. "I've been making bowls my whole life and it still amazes me each time I finish one."

Jed spoke up, "How did you make the tiny holes all over it? We never saw you do that."

"The holes?" he asked, as a wrinkled grin appeared on his face. "I didn't put the holes in the bowl," he said it as if he thought maybe they had put the holes there.

The boys both turned to Mr. Griswold and Cal said, "Well, who did?" trying to figure it out before he got his answer.

"God did," Mr. Griswold said. The boys pictured God coming into the shop at night.

"When did he do it?" Cal asked.

"Oh, He's been working on it for a long time," Mr. Griswold answered. The boys were confused and Mr. Griswold knew that he was going to have to explain it from the beginning. "You see, we made this bowl from a burl. The burl is a big knot on a tree that grows and grows, leaving tiny spots of decayed bark inside. You can't really see them until you cut it open," he said. "When we carved the bowl, it revealed all the ugly spots in the wood. Matter of fact, the beauty of the bowl isn't the wood itself but the ugly spots revealed by me, the bowl maker." He stopped to let that sink in and then he said as he gestured to the bowl, "I guess that's what I like most about carving these bowls... it reminds me of ME...and Christmas."

"What do you mean?" Jed said.

"Well, God doesn't just choose the most beautiful people, or the smartest people, or even the most talented people to love. He mostly chooses plain, ordinary folks, like me—real people, who have real struggles, real problems, and some real painful failures. It's like the wood we chose for your mom's Christmas bowl. You probably wouldn't have chosen that burl…it certainly isn't much to look at from the outside. You would have chosen a piece of wood that looked good on the outside and overlooked the burl. But I knew differently.

I knew what kind of bowl it could be. I knew that all those imperfections are what make the bowl beautiful. That's why this bowl reminds me of ME and Christmas, because I know what God did in my life. I am like the burl—plain, ugly, and rotting, and I made a lot of mistakes in life, but those same mistakes, taken and molded in God's hands, are what makes me beautiful.

A tear trickled down Mr. Griswold's cheek as he smiled, turned to Jed, muffed up his hair, and then stood tall and straight. "That's what Christmas is all about. God chose plain, ordinary shepherds, humble parents, and a dirty, old stable in which to reveal His Son to the world. He still uses regular people who need Him to work in their lives. God doesn't take the mistakes and failures away…He makes them beautiful. That's why He sent His son…that's why we have Christmas."

"Bring your dad over tomorrow," he said, changing the subject, "and you can take your Mom's Christmas bowl home." The boys looked at the bowl one more time and then hurried out the barn door to return home.

The next day, all three of them came to the door as they had that very first day, except this time the boys weren't the least bit nervous. Mr. Griswold came to the door and invited them in, although the boys were already through the door and standing by the workbench near the finished bowl.

"Wow, that's the most beautiful bowl I've ever seen!" their dad exclaimed.

"Yep, it sure is," Mr. Griswold responded. Cal and Jed danced in the excitement of the moment. They knew their dad would like the bowl and he did. After staring at it for a moment, their dad asked in his nervous voice, "How much do I owe you, Mr. Griswold?"

Mr. Griswold looked a little confused and said without hesitation, "Why, you already paid."

"No, I didn't," their Dad said, thinking Mr. Griswold was confused, him being old and everything. Mr. Griswold spoke in a calm voice. "Yes, you did, by allowing your two boys to help me for so many days. I can't remember when I had so much fun. I enjoyed every minute I got to spend with them." The boys would have been flattered by his words if they had heard them, but they were too busy playing with some wood shavings on the shop floor.

"I don't know what to say," their dad said. "Thank you so much." Mr. Griswold placed the bowl in a grocery sack and they walked from the barn towards their car.

"Oh, I forgot one thing," Mr. Griswold said in a startled voice. He darted back into the barn and a moment later returned carrying two sticks in his hands. "Caleb and

Jedidiah, these are yours." He held out their carved walking sticks and the brothers looked at their Dad to see if it was okay to take them.

"Go on, boys," their dad said. They ran to Mr. Griswold and took the sticks from his hands.

It was then that Cal asked nervously, "Do you think it'd be okay if we came over to help you on other bowls?"

Mr. Griswold smiled and said, "I can't think of anything I'd like better…as long as it's okay with your dad."

The boys turned in relief and ran off to the car, their carved walking sticks in hand, and waved to Mr. Griswold.

"Merry Christmas!" he called after them.

"Merry Christmas, Mr. Griswold!" they yelled back.

Later that evening while their mom was folding some laundry, all three of boys wrapped the bowl in brightly colored Christmas paper and placed it deep under the tree.

A few days later on Christmas morning, after every other gift had been opened, their dad said to his boys, "I think there is one more…for Mom to open." Cal and Jed looked at each other and then handed their mother the special present. They watched in excitement as she pulled back the wrapping paper and held the Christmas bowl in her hands. It glistened in the glow of the tree.

A smile spread over her face and she said, "This is the most beautiful bowl I've ever seen." She hugged everyone in the room and the two boys told her about their adventure with Mr. Griswold, how the bowl was made, how the little holes were made, and what they meant.

Over the years, the boys often found themselves at Mr. Griswold's working on bowls for other customers, sweeping the floor, or walking through the woods in search of just the right piece of wood. And the Christmas bowl? Each year after Thanksgiving, it was carefully pulled from the top shelf in the kitchen and proudly displayed in the middle of the dining room table filled with pine cones or ornaments for all to see.

Years later, after Cal and Jed had moved away and gotten married and Mr. Griswold had died, they would come visit their folks with families of their own at Christmas. Before the last suitcase would be brought in, they would stop and at look at the Christmas bowl, run their fingers against its smooth sides, examine the tiny dark holes in its surface, and remember Mr. Griswold and his smile.

And when one of their children would ask, "How did he make the tiny holes?" they'd hold the bowl up to their children's faces just like Mr. Griswold did when they were boys and tell them of Christmas and how God still takes people with past mistakes, failures, and heartache and crafts them into something beautiful for all to see.

"Mr. Griswold taught us that," they'd say with a smile, remembering their adventure and the year of the Christmas Bowl.

The End

THE CHRISTMAS GAME FOR THE ENTIRE FAMILY!

Make playing the "To Bethlehem" Game a part of your family's Christmas traditions!

Be the first to reach the Newborn King . . .but beware, there'll be expenses along the way! Each player starts out with 5 shekels as they attempt to make their way to Bethlehem. Along the way, they'll have to complete zany activities, spend some shekels, and answer "Around the Campfire" questions about their own favorite Christmas traditions, memories, and other holiday thoughts. With a number of fun options, and Roman plastic coins to play with, this is one game your kids might beg to play year-round! Includes instructions, cards, Roman plastic coins, and 10 player pieces.